SECOND CHANCE SUMMER

KAIT NOLAN

TAKE THE LEAP PUBLISHING

Second Chance Summer

Written and published by Kait Nolan

Copyright 2017 Kait Nolan

Cover design by Lori Jackson

AUTHOR'S NOTE: The following is a work of fiction. All people, places, and events are purely products of the author's imagination. Any resemblance to actual people, places, or events is entirely coincidental.

For all the recovering academics out there...there's life beyond the university! Don't forget to live it.

A LETTER TO READERS

Dear Reader,

This book also contains swearing and pre-marital sex between the lead couple, as those things are part of the realistic lives of characters of this generation, and of many of my readers.

If any of these things are not your cup of tea, please consider that you may not be the right audience for this book. There are scores of other books out there that are written with you in mind. In fact, I've got a list of some of my favorite authors who write on the sweeter side on my website at https://kaitnolan.com/on-the-sweeter-side/

If you choose to stick with me, I hope you enjoy!

Happy reading!

Kait

CHAPTER 1

"I'VE NEVER SEEN ANYBODY so excited to ride a bus before."

Audrey Graham gave a little bounce on the vinyl-covered bench seat, strangely delighted with the squeak of springs. "I've never been on one. I mean, not a school bus. Just the public transit kind."

Beside her, Samantha Ferguson, her partner in this adventure, chuckled and grabbed hold of the seat in front of them for balance as the bus lurched through a pot hole. "Whatever floats your boat, sugar."

"If you're looking for an authentic school bus ride, I can always start a spitball fight." This came from the guy who'd twisted around from the next seat up. The mop of sandy hair and smattering of freckles across his cheeks made him look several years younger than he probably was. He stuck out a hand. "Charlie."

Was this what camp was like? All first names all the time? It was so different from the formality and pretentiousness of academia.

"Audrey. And this is Sam." They all shook hands.

"Where are you from?" Charlie asked.

"Little bitty town in northeast Tennessee called Eden's Ridge," Sam replied. "Though most recently Chattanooga. I teach at a small, private college there. So does Audrey."

For now. "I'm originally from Kansas City, though."

"Long Island. I work in Manhattan these days."

"Yeah? What do you do?" Audrey asked, unable to imagine this golden retriever of a man amid the stiff suits and stuffed shirts.

"I'm an assistant editor at Macmillan."

Sam brightened. "Yeah? What genre?"

"Don't laugh. Romance."

"Now you've done it," Audrey warned. "The book monster has awoken. Sam's an English Lit professor and romance aficionado."

"Really? I'd have thought you'd turn your nose up at romance."

"No way. I love it. I even teach a class on the development of the genre and its relation to feminist theory."

Audrey hid a smile as the two launched into an animated discussion of favorite authors. She had no idea if there were any prospective sparks there, but at least Sam had found a kindred spirit.

"Are you two returning campers to Camp Firefly Falls?" Charlie's question pulled her attention back to the conversation.

"First timers," Sam told him. "Audrey here is a summer camp virgin."

Audrey felt her cheeks heat with a blush and had no idea why. It wasn't like she was *that* kind of virgin.

Not exactly far off... her brain reminded her.

Shut up.

"No shit? Well, the Retro Session is definitely the way to go to get the experience," Charlie said. "I came here every summer, when I was a kid. Got super pumped when I found out it'd been turned into a camp for grown-ups."

"Me too I'm tackling some entries on my bucket list lately, and when I heard about Camp Firefly Falls, it seemed like an opportunity to knock a few out in one fell swoop." Which was the most understated way Audrey could possibly explain her reasons for being here. But spilling her guts to a complete stranger on the camp bus as they drove up from New York was not one of those bucket list items.

"So you've never been to camp, and you went to camp somewhere else?" Charlie asked, looking from Audrey to Sam.

"Hale River Camp and Farm, in North Alabama," Sam replied.

"That's a long way from the Berkshires. How'd you hear about Camp Firefly Falls?"

The flash of phantom pain in her legs kept Audrey from answering immediately. Riding the wave, she forced a smile. "Oh, someone I met once mentioned coming here as a kid. I guess the name stuck in my head."

"I'm just along for the ride and to get my nostalgia on," Sam put in. "I *loved* camp. Went every year, from the time I was seven— camper through counselor."

She and Charlie fell back into easy conversation, and Audrey let them, focusing instead on breathing through the ache. The novelty of the bus ride was wearing thin. She'd been sitting too long and her legs were beginning to cramp up. A walk would be in order as soon as they got their stuff dumped at the cabin. Maybe a stroll along Lake Waawaatesi. It had looked so picturesque in the promo photos online.

From the back of the bus, someone began to sing "She'll Be Comin' Round The Mountain" as they turned onto the long, winding road that would, according to the map Audrey had studied, lead up to Camp Firefly Falls. They were nearly there. Then she'd have two, long, glorious weeks with no cell phone, no email, no reminders of the career decisions she still needed to make. Two weeks to relax. Two weeks to take life by the horns and really live it. Which meant pushing herself out of her comfort zone. She'd become an expert at pushing herself the last two years. More than she ought to, according to her parents, but what did they know? If she'd listened to them, she wouldn't have anything resembling a life anymore.

Well, okay, that wasn't entirely fair. They meant well. They'd always meant well. But it was her life, and she was finally going to live it. Going to camp was just the latest in a long line of small rebellions. Who knew that she, of all people, would develop a taste for defiance at the ripe old age of twenty-seven? But was it enough to change her life over? That was part of what she was here to figure out. Maybe, by the end of session, she'd finally know what she wanted.

Abruptly, the lush green trees opened up and the bus turned beneath an arched sign that read *Camp Firefly Falls*.

"We're here!" Audrey couldn't keep the excitement from her voice.

A cheer swept the bus as they pulled into a gravel parking lot, where a blonde woman with a pony tail stood behind a folding card table, surrounded by a handful of staff members in Camp Firefly Falls t-shirts. Audrey was on her feet the moment they rolled to a stop. Her legs protested the rapid movement, and she had to grab Charlie's seat to catch her balance.

Sam slipped an arm around Audrey's waist to steady her. "Okay?"

"Just stiff. Let's get out."

They edged into the aisle and filed off the bus with the other campers. A couple of other staff members circled around to the back and began offloading luggage as Audrey, Sam, and the others got in a loose line at the table to register and pick up their cabin assignments.

"Hi!" The blonde offered up a wide smile. "I'm Heather Tully. My husband and I own the camp. Welcome!"

"We're so excited to be here. I'm Audrey Graham, and this is Samantha Ferguson."

"Excellent. You're in Cabin 7."

"Lucky number," Sam pronounced.

If this were one of the camp movies Audrey had binge watched before coming, some guy would make a crude joke about getting lucky in Cabin 7. Apparently, the Camp Firefly Falls alums were a little more discreet. Or maybe real life was less salacious than the movies.

"Now, if you'll just turn in your cell phones. We'll keep them locked up at the lodge, so no worries something might happen to them." Heather held out zip top bags with their names scrawled out in marker.

"No cell phones?" Sam asked, digging in her purse.

"It's a new rule we're trying out for the Retro Session. Cell phones weren't a thing back when we were kids at camp, and we're trying to get back to that feel as much as we can."

"Sign me up. I can't remember the last time I went a day without hearing a phone ring." Sam slipped her phone into the bag.

Audrey sent one last text off to her mom. **Arrived at camp safely. No phones allowed. I'll talk to you in two weeks.** Then she powered down and slid her phone into the other bag. Two whole weeks where her parents couldn't pressure her about Berkeley. That sounded like heaven.

Heather pulled out a map for each of them and circled Cabin 7. "If you head just up that trail and take the left fork, past the dining hall, you'll find your cabin ready and waiting. Dinner's going to be served at six, and we're having a little opening night mixer at the boat house starting at seven-thirty. Come ready to dance!"

Audrey took her map. "We'll be there with bells on."

AT THE SIGHT of the bus turning onto the final road to Camp Firefly Falls, Hudson Lowell grimaced. The last thing he wanted was to get caught up in the crazy of drop off day with all the other campers. Was it even called drop off day now that they were all adults? Didn't matter. Either way, there'd be enough excitement and good cheer that he'd be liable to deck somebody. Better to kill a little time and circle back. There'd be no avoiding the walk down memory lane the next two weeks, but he could ease into it rather than leaping feet first. So, he drove on past the turn and kept heading north, wondering if Boone's was still in business.

Part gas station, part general store, part diner, Boone's had always been an official stop before his parents dropped him off to camp as a kid. Located halfway between camp and Briarsted, the nearest town, Boone's was the last bastion of civilization before two weeks of unfettered, summertime awesome. Ten minutes later, he pulled his Jeep into the lot. The whole complex was smaller than he'd remembered, but the scent of freshly brewed coffee was the same. It drew him back into the diner, where he settled into a booth and grabbed the laminated menu from between the napkin holder and the ketchup. He looked at the options without much interest.

A gum-chewing waitress appeared at the table, a pot of coffee in her hand. "What can I getcha, hon?"

"Just coffee. And a slice of pie." Pie was always a good idea.

She turned over the cup at his elbow and filled it near to the brim. "Apple or peach?"

"Peach. With ice cream."

"Comin' right up."

As she disappeared, Hudson slipped his phone out. Might as well make this last call before he got on up the mountain. Reception would probably be spotty.

"Hudson!"

"Hey Mom."

"Are you there yet? Is it fabulous? I'm so curious what all they've done to change the place since you were a boy."

He gritted his teeth against her cheer. "I haven't quite made it to camp yet. I stopped in at Boone's."

She laughed "Of course. Couldn't go to camp for two weeks without your Twizzlers."

Had he even had a Twizzler in the past decade?

The waitress returned with his pie a la mode, and Hudson nodded his thanks.

"I just wanted to check-in one last time, before I got up there. Cell coverage will probably be lousy. You've got the number to the camp office, in case you need to reach me for anything." Translation: In case there's any change in John's condition.

"Got it right here. But sweetheart, I really want you to give this a chance. Embrace the whole camp experience. You used to have such fun up there. Unplugging from things will be good for you."

Unplugging. An unfortunate word choice. Hudson closed his eyes as his brain conjured the tone of a flatlining heart monitor. His hand fisted around the fork. "Yeah. I'll try."

By the time he got off the phone, he'd lost whatever appetite he'd had for the pie. He ate it anyway, a mechanical shoveling in of food that had become habit the past few months. Food was necessary fuel, whether you tasted it or not. Leaving some cash on the table to pay his bill, he gassed up the Jeep. Then, remembering the promise to his mother, he bought a couple of packs of Twizzlers for nostalgia's sake and got back on the road to camp.

The bus crowd had cleared out. A lone blonde with a pony tail sat at the registration table. She looked up at his approach and broke into a grin. "Why Hudson Lowell. Didn't you grow up nice?"

"Don't know about nice, but I grew up. So'd you. Heard you married Michael."

"I did. We run this place together."

"Suits you," Hudson said. Heather Hawn had been one of his first camp crushes, but she'd never had eyes for anybody but Michael Tully. She looked happy. The kind of down-to-the-bone happy that exhausted him just from looking.

She checked her clipboard. "You're in Cabin 16 with Charlie

Thayer. He got here about an hour ago from New York. You're in Syracuse these days?"

"I am."

Seeming to sense his reticence to talk, Heather turned all businesslike. "Not that I think you'll need it, but here's a map of camp and our list of available activities. Dinner's at six, and we're having an opening night dance at the boat house at seven-thirty."

He'd rather be shot. But he took the handouts and thanked her before turning toward the Jeep for his gear.

"Oh, Hudson, I'll need your phone."

"Sorry?"

"We're banning them for the Retro Session. This is a technology-free zone."

"Not happening, Heather."

"You don't strike me as the type who'd be addicted to Candy Crush."

"I've got family in the hospital. They need to be able to reach me if things take a turn for the worse."

Her smile faded. "Oh, I'm so sorry. Well, keep it, then. But I'll warn you, reception is spotty, at best."

"Noted."

Charlie—whom he had dim memories of from years before as someone they'd short-sheeted once—wasn't at the cabin when Hudson arrived, though he'd already claimed the right side for his own. The cabin was still rustic in appearance, but the Tullys had done quite a bit more than spruce the place up. Instead of the old-school bunk beds with room to sleep eight, there were only two twin beds with quality mattresses, already made up with real bedding instead of lying bare and waiting for a sleeping bag. Hudson shoved the one he'd brought beneath the bed. The bathroom was small, but functional, with hotel-style towels and travel-size toiletries. They definitely hadn't had AC back in the day. Curious despite himself, he headed out to see what else had changed in the past seventeen years.

The lodge was the most obvious difference. A grand structure of wood and stone, he'd read that it now housed five-star dining with an honest-to-God chef in residence, along with conference rooms, staff quarters, and luxury suites. Hudson guessed there was a market for those kinds of amenities, but he hoped there'd be some straight up burgers cooked over a campfire while he was here. He was more a pot of chili kind of guy, or he could go for a vat of spaghetti, served family-style around the long table at the firehouse. Not that he'd been doing any of that lately either.

They'd added a ropes course—a big, sprawling labyrinth of ropes and platforms. It was the kind of setup that looked more intimidating than it actually was. Climbers would be strapped into harnesses and attached to guide wires the entire time. Probably the liability insurance for the place wouldn't allow for anything else. But still, he'd check that out, at some point. Maybe he'd see if they had gear for some rock climbing, too. That kind of physical exertion suited his desire to push himself to exhaustion in hopes of maybe sleeping. He might not be out with his company, but he'd kept himself in top shape since he recovered from the fall.

The wooded trails crisscrossing the grounds felt the same as did the long pier that branched off to the boat house. Hudson could see racks of kayaks and canoes. He followed the pull toward the water. The gentle lap of it against the wooden pilings soothed his nerves a bit. He had definite plans to grab one of those kayaks and disappear. There were countless inlets to explore along the length of Lake Waawaatesi. He might even do some fishing while he was here. Fish didn't talk or expect you to talk back. He figured that made for much better therapy.

As he started to turn back toward camp proper, he caught a flash of fire. A woman strolled along the bank on the other side of the lake, her face tipped up to the sunshine, a gorgeous fall of red hair rippling in the breeze. From this distance, Hudson couldn't see her face, but he knew she was smiling. Everything about her posture suggested absolute peace. He found himself watching until she disappeared into the trees.

Shaking off the vague ripple of envy, Hudson decided to curtail the rest of his tour. Better to unpack and settle in before dinner, get a little quiet. He'd have to deal with people soon enough.

CHAPTER 2

"WELCOME TO OUR RETRO Session at Camp Firefly Falls!"

Cheers practically raised the roof of the boathouse. Strands of twinkle lights were wrapped up the columns and around the rafters, giving the whole place a party vibe. The general jubilation of the campers added to the effect. Up on the little stage, Heather grinned from ear to ear. "Tonight kicks off two weeks of turning back the clock. We've got all your favorite, classic camp activities." She listed off several options Audrey remembered seeing in the brochure. "—with a few more grown up options thrown in." She gestured toward the bar that had been set up to one side of the dance floor. "My husband, Michael, is playing bartender tonight. We remind you to have fun and please drink responsibly. That said, let's get this party started!"

The sound system rocked out with "Here's To Never Growing Up" and people exploded onto the floor.

Audrey hadn't expected quite this level of chaos. She leaned toward Sam, raising her voice to be heard over the music. "Is this a normal camp thing?"

"Don't know about here. Hale River had dances, but nothing like this."

"This is a Camp Firefly Falls dance on steroids," Charlie said.

"Let's get out there!" Sam gave a little hop in time with the chorus.

"You two go ahead. I'm going to get a drink." With a drink, she'd have reason to stay outside the chaos and observe. No way would her legs allow for dancing. Not after today.

Sam gave her two thumbs up and dove after Charlie into the gyrating crowd. Was this what a mosh pit was like?

Audrey edged her way around the floor, watching and absorbing body language, automatically analyzing with her scientist's mind. It seemed a lot of these people knew each other. From what she'd heard, this was as much a reunion as a throw-back session, so that made sense.

What must that be like? To have friends you made as a child that either stayed with you for years, or who you could pick back up with after all this time passed as if it were yesterday. Audrey couldn't imagine that. She had friends, of course. Plenty of them as an adult. But as a child, she'd been painfully self-conscious, shy, and so far above her peers intellectually they hadn't been able to relate to her at all. She'd been weird. Awkward. A freak. It had been easy to retreat into her studies.

School was easy. School followed some sense of logic and rules, and her academic performance had delighted her parents. Continuing along that track had just made sense. College. Grad school. Going into research professionally had been a no brainer. Audrey had an aptitude, and, in the Graham family, ignoring that would've been considered a crime. Over the years, she'd quietly amassed a list of all the life experiences she'd missed out on because of a lifetime spent worshiping at the altar of academia—never with any clear idea what she was going to do with it. It was more as a form of observational research. After the accident, that list had become her Holy Grail.

"Hi there."

Audrey slid her gaze up to the guy who'd paused beside her. He was attractive in a clean cut, Ivy League sort of way, with the kind of confidence she'd seen often during her stint at Yale. The jeans and Camp Firefly Falls t-shirt he wore saved him from being unapproachable. She wondered where she could get one of those and made a mental note to track down one of the staff to ask.

"I'm Brad."

The correct social convention is to speak. Open your mouth, she ordered herself. "Audrey."

"Want to dance, Audrey?"

A refusal was on the tip of her tongue, but the music shifted into something less energetic. Something by Jack Johnson. No: a slow song, exactly, but something she could get away with not bouncing around to. Number thirty-seven on her list was *Attend a school dance.* This was probably as close as she'd ever get. She worked up a smile. "Sure."

Brad knew how to dance. That much was obvious when she put her hand in his and followed him out onto the floor. His grip on her was light but sure. Audrey forced herself to relax and follow his lead.

"First time at Camp Firefly Falls?" he asked.

"What gave me away?"

"The way you're watching everybody, like you're not quite sure what to do."

Audrey tried not to take offense at that since it was true. "I expected something a little more low-key tonight."

"Kumbaya and s'mores?"

Number fifty-four: Roast marshmallows over a real campfire to make authentic s'mores. That had to be better than roasting them over the burner of the gas range in her apartment.

"Well, I did have my heart set on s'mores."

"They have a campfire for that purpose every night, so if that's what your heart desires, we can absolutely make that happen." He flashed a too-practiced smile.

Was he flirting with her? Or just being friendly? This was one of those areas of human behavior she'd never felt comfortable assessing with any kind of accuracy. Uncertain, she gave a half smile and continued to watch the people around them. Probably it was rude not to maintain eye contact, but that felt too intimate. She didn't know what to say to this guy.

Brad's grip shifted. Before she could ask what that was about, he was whipping her out into a spin. At least, that's what she assumed he was trying to do. Her legs couldn't keep up, crossing over themselves like a pretzel, making her stumble. Pain shot up from her ankles, through her knees. Shock and an instant panic kept her from crying out. But his quick reflexes kept her from falling or from crashing into the couples dancing nearby.

"Whoops. Sorry about that. Didn't mean to surprise you."

Audrey held onto him, not because she wanted to but because without his support, she was pretty sure she'd drop like a stone.

"Audrey, you okay?" The concern in his voice told her she hadn't managed to hide the wince.

"I think I twisted my ankle." She hadn't, but it was the easiest explanation that would get her off the dance floor.

"Crap, I'm so sorry. Here, let me help you." He led her over to a row of chairs near the bar. "Should I find the camp doctor?"

She waved him off. "No need. I'll be fine. I'm just going to sit here a bit. You go on and keep dancing."

"You're sure I can't do anything?"

He looked so distressed at the idea that he'd ruined her evening, she relented. "Grab me a glass of wine?"

"I can do that. What kind?"

"Anything red."

He brought her a glass of merlot and, after much urging, returned to the dancing. Audrey let out a long, controlled breath, imagining the pain leaving with the exhale. Sometimes that worked. Sometimes it didn't. She'd have a date later with some muscle rub and the cold packs she'd shoved into the freezer of their mini fridge on arrival. She took a sip of her drink and relaxed in the chair. At least the wine was excellent.

Someone stepped up to the bar behind her. "Beer."

Audrey cocked her head at the word, not knowing why.

"What kind?" Michael reeled off several types.

"The IPA." There was something about that voice. It was deep, the kind of resonant timbre that soaked into your skin.

Come on. Say more than two words.

She heard ice shifting as Michael dug through the cooler. "You settling in okay? Got everything you need?"

"Yeah." A pause, as if the speaker were taking a pull on the beer. "It's a lot swankier than I remember."

Michael laughed and said something in return, but Audrey didn't hear it. His response, the music, the pain in her legs, everything else faded as her mind zeroed in on the other guy. She *knew* that voice. Had dreamed of it over and over. Had heard it in her head, urging her on through all the grueling months of physical therapy.

Or maybe it was just that she wanted it to be him. Her nameless savior.

She turned around, hoping the sight of his face would jog her memory, but he'd already left the bar and was striding across the boathouse. He didn't stop to speak to anyone, didn't even acknowledge other campers were there. He just walked on out the door and into the night.

Before she could change her mind, Audrey shoved to her feet and followed.

~

COMING BACK to Camp Firefly Falls had been a mistake. But Hudson's mom had been so hopeful when they'd presented the trip to him—a surprise for the birthday he'd rather not have acknowledged. Some peace and quiet and fun was just what he needed. Right.

Sadly, only one person could give him what he needed, and right now the fucker wasn't cooperating. Goddamned coma.

Hudson's cabinmate had somehow managed to convince him to show up at the mixer without earning a fist in the face. Charlie had the kind of unwavering good cheer that Hudson didn't know how to fight against, at least not without feeling like he'd kicked a puppy. So, he'd come and immediately wished he were anywhere else. At least there was beer. He'd lasted two songs before he couldn't take any more of the shiny, happy people or the blasting of the music. The thump of it followed him out to the end of the pier, but it wasn't so suffocating standing at the edge of Lake Waawaatesi. Just him and his beer and the night. No reason to let his foul mood spill over onto anyone else.

The sound of someone's hesitant footsteps on the dock had him tensing. Whether it was somebody from the old days or just a party goer looking to play Get To Know You, he wanted none of it. Talking was the last thing he felt like doing. He was already calculating where he could disappear to get the fuck away from people when a quiet voice spoke behind him.

"Excuse me."

Be polite, asshole.

Taking a breath, Hudson turned to find a petite redhead. The same one he'd seen on the other side of the lake this afternoon? She was a pretty little thing, looking out of place in her pants and flowy top amid all the camp t-shirts and shorts.

She stared at him for long moments with an intensity that surprised him, as if she were looking past his face to somewhere deeper. It was unnerving. Then her serious face lightened. "It *is* you."

Okay, not what he'd been expecting. "I'm sorry? Do we know each other?" Surely, he'd remember a face like that.

"I—no. Not really. You don't recognize me, do you?" She gave a self-deprecatory laugh, as if the very idea that he might was stupid. "No, of course you wouldn't. I'm not covered in blood this time."

That got his attention.

"You saved my life," she continued.

Hudson looked back now, really looked, mentally visualizing that face streaked with blood. Something about that macabre image snapped a memory into focus. "I-81."

"Yes."

He tried to remember the details. The accident had been about two years ago. One of the worst car crashes he'd ever worked. Even with the Jaws of Life, it had taken more than an hour to get her out of the car, and when they had...

"You're walking."

She beamed at that. "I am. The doctors said I wouldn't, but I'm more stubborn than they are."

"That's amazing." And he meant it. Her legs had been a bloody, mangled mess. Hudson couldn't imagine what she must've gone through to get to this point.

They lapsed into silence. As the moment stretched out from one to two, to more than a dozen, she knotted her hands in obvious discomfort.

"I just...I heard your voice. In there." She gestured back toward the boat house. "And I remembered. I don't remember a lot of the accident..."

That was a blessing. He didn't know much about what had caused the accident, just that by the time he'd gotten to the scene, her car was more-or-less fused with an eighteen-wheeler and a mini-van and there were two fatalities. He'd been determined she wouldn't be the third.

"Anyway, I just had to see if it was really you."

"Guess it is." What were the odds that this woman he'd rescued from a mangled car with out-of-state plates would be here, now, at Camp Firefly Falls of all places?

"I never had a chance to thank you. I wouldn't be alive today, if it weren't for you."

Hudson felt something twist in his chest at the claim. "I was just doing my job. If it hadn't been me, it'd have been someone else."

"But it wasn't someone else. It was you. And maybe it was your job, but you did it damned well. You kept me calm and distracted, when I was in unspeakable pain. And you got me out." Something rippled over her face—a remembered pain? The fear?

He remembered her terror, barely kept at bay as her body went into shock. Remembered, too, the talking, talking, talking to try to keep her mind on anything else. The idea that that was still with her—and why wouldn't it be?—bothered him, made him want to do...something.

"Look, you got me out, and I wanted to...can I..." She shifted, dropping her gaze for a moment before bringing it back to his. "Okay maybe this is stupid, but can I just give you a hug?" Her voice was a little scratchy as she said it, and even in the darkness, he could see the stain of color in her cheeks.

Everything in Hudson wanted to step back. This was all way too close to *feeling shit,* and he had plenty of his own to deal with. But he also knew it would be a complete dick move not to grant her this one, small request.

"Sure." He set his beer on one of the rope-wrapped pilings.

Her expression eased.

He expected some awkward little dance, while they tried to figure out how to get past being basically strangers. Instead, she stepped into him without hesitation, sliding her arms around his waist and squeezing tight. She was a good bit shorter than he was, and her head nestled just right against his chest, somewhere in the vicinity of the heart he'd tried to shut off.

His arms lifted, wrapping around her shoulders, one hand

cradling her head as he hugged her back because... He didn't know why, except that it felt damned good and nothing had felt good in months.

"Thank you," she whispered.

She pressed her cheek to his heart and sighed, a long exhale of tension that seemed to pull some of his own out with it. He stood with this virtual stranger in his arms and wondered if he ought to be the one thanking her.

CHAPTER 3

*T*HANKING HER RESCUER WAS possibly the most important thing on Audrey's list. To finally be able to do it, even if she couldn't really express what it meant to her, felt amazing. So did being in his arms. She'd expected a perfunctory squeeze, at most. But he'd hugged her back, and what had been meant as a simple thank you had turned into an embrace. Had she ever really let anyone hold her? Not like this. This whole thing had gone on way longer than she'd intended because...well, he seemed to need it. She knew grief and pain, and she'd recognized it in his face. If a simple hug would help even a little bit, who was she to deny him?

He seemed to register the weirdness a few moments after she did. They broke apart, an awkward disentangling of limbs. Audrey didn't know what to do. She'd said what she needed to say. She didn't really want to go back to the dance, but he obviously came out here because he didn't want company. Maybe she'd go find Sam and beg off the rest of the evening. Retreat to the cabin and ice her legs.

"Audrey," he said. "Your name is Audrey."

Something warm and fuzzy bloomed in her chest. He remembered her name. "Audrey Graham. I'm sorry, I never knew your name."

"Hudson Lowell."

"Nice to meet you, Hudson." After another beat of awkward silence, she started to turn.

"You wanna sit?"

The question surprised her. She looked around but saw no chairs. If she sat on the dock, she might not be able to get up again. But despite the risk, she didn't want to leave him. This man who had haunted her dreams for two years. The chance to find out more about the real guy was too good to pass up. "Sure."

Hudson retrieved his beer, toed off his shoes, and dropped down to the edge of the pier, dipping his feet into the water.

Audrey hesitated. "Isn't it cold?"

"Little bit."

Well, maybe this would serve the same purpose as icing. Using his shoulder for balance, she carefully lowered herself. He knew what she'd been through, so there was no sense in hiding the fact that she needed a little help. She pulled off her shoes and socks and tugged up the wide legs of her pants just far enough they wouldn't get wet. Despite the darkness, she was still paranoid about her scars. Knowing and seeing were two very different things.

The water was frigid and perfect, the coolness immediately starting to alleviate the ache. She flexed her toes and feet, slowly rotating her ankles.

He dangled the longneck bottle between two fingers, looking out over the lake. "How did you end up at Camp Firefly Falls?"

Audrey glanced over at him. "Because of you, actually."

"Me?" That pulled his attention back to her.

"You talked about it when you were cutting me out. I guess it stuck." She shrugged with a nonchalance she didn't feel. "The accident was a kind of wakeup call for me. I'd been putting all this focus on my career, practically since kindergarten—" Which was only a slight exaggeration. "—and I realized I'd been putting off actual living. Once I could do stuff again, I decided to start making up for lost time. I never got to go to camp as a kid, so when I found out they did grown-up camp and had a two-week retro session, I signed up."

"What is it you do?"

"I'm a professor."

Hudson gave her the side eye. "You seem kinda young for that."

She rolled her eyes heavenward, thankful that she was old enough now that not every single person she met had that reaction. "I finished my PhD at twenty-three."

"Seriously?"

"Seriously."

He digested that for a moment. "So, you were...how old when you finished high school?"

"I graduated a few months before I turned sixteen."

"Holy shit."

She shrugged again, wishing they could talk about anything else but how much of a freak she was. "I skipped a few grades." She waited for the intimidation or the interrogation about how smart she was. It was what people generally did when they found out.

Instead he surprised her. "That must've been hard. Being so out-of-sync age-wise with your classmates." It was an insightful observation and absolutely true.

"Yeah. I kind of skipped a lot of normal kid rites of passage."

"Hence camp."

"Hence camp," she agreed.

He tipped back his beer. "Well, for an authentic camp experience, you need a number of components."

Her mouth pulled into a smile. "Should I be taking notes?"

"Reckon you'd be good at that after all that school."

"True enough. So, the requisite components for an authentic camp experience?"

"You got your water sports, woodsy stuff, crafty stuff—I always avoided that like the plague, except for that one summer I had a crush on Jennifer Saylor and sat through macramé for two whole days because I thought she might notice me."

"Did she?"

"Sadly, no. *She* had a thing for Pete Zimmerman, who was a counselor-in-training at the time."

"So, you suffered through macramé for nothing?"

"Not nothing. I took home a real nice plant hammock to my mom."

Audrey giggled.

He continued to talk about all the different activities, ranking the stuff she really needed to try while she was here. And it was fun, sitting here with him, talking about camp, and flirting. She was pretty sure this was flirting. He told more stories about his summers at Camp Firefly Falls, entertaining her with various hijinks. He seemed to relax a little more with each story, until she could almost forget the grief she'd seen in his eyes earlier. She wanted to ask if he'd show her some of these places and activities, because she wanted to spend some more time with him, but that was still a little too far outside her comfort zone. Right now, it was enough to sit here with him as their toes turned pruney.

Behind them the dance was breaking up. People began to stream out of the boathouse, headed back to their cabins or to the nightly campfire.

Hudson looked over his shoulder. "Maybe we ought to call it a night."

Audrey hoped her disappointment didn't show. "Guess it is getting kinda late."

"Can I walk you back to your cabin?"

"That'd be nice."

He boosted himself up in a fluid motion that had her wishing it was daylight and he was in nothing but board shorts so she could see the easy flex of muscle that enabled him to do that. That was definitely on her wish list of camp memories. Maybe later in the week.

Shifting, Audrey tried to lift her legs out of the water and realized she couldn't get up. After all the sitting on the bus and the sitting on the hard pier for however long they'd been out here, her legs simply refused to work.

Damn it.

For the last hour or so, she'd managed to forget she was damaged. He'd made her feel normal. Just a woman, chatting and flirting with an interesting, sexy guy. The last thing she wanted was to remind him that she was anything but.

HUDSON SLIPPED his sandals back on.

From where she still sat, Audrey burst out, "You know what? I think I'll sit out here a while longer. You go ahead."

She wouldn't look at him, but he could still see the flags of color in her cheeks, the hunch of her shoulders. Had he said something wrong? Mentally reviewing their conversation, he couldn't pinpoint anything, but hell, he was so out of practice having a normal conversation these days, how would he know?

Never one to push a woman, he shoved his hands in his pockets. "Okay, I'll see you around."

"Night, Hudson." There was something odd in her tone.

Not your business, he told himself.

He made it to the end of the dock before he looked back. She was dragging herself backward with her hands, maneuvering herself out of the water entirely with her upper body. Hudson cursed long and low for not realizing she was having trouble with her legs. She'd needed him for balance to sit down. Why wouldn't she need a hand up?

He jogged back to her. "Are you in pain?"

Audrey dropped her face into her hands, the flush creeping up the back of her neck. "God." She still wouldn't look at him. "No. Not really, they're just...asleep." Her voice was strangled as if she couldn't bear for him to see her weakness. "They'll wake up in a minute."

Not so long as she was sitting on the hard pier. Hudson scooped her up.

Audrey gave a surprised squeak. "What are you doing?"

"Which cabin are you in?"

"Seven. You can't just carry me all the way back to my cabin."

"Watch me. Here, grab your shoes." He bent so she could reach them, then simply curled her close against his chest and started walking. She weighed more than she looked, but he was willing to bet there was a fair amount of metal in her legs now. Not that he'd ask. Either way, she was nothing compared to the hoses and firefighting gear he lugged around on a daily basis.

"People are staring," she hissed.

He'd noticed that and didn't much care, but at the distress in her tone, he skirted the remainder of the crowd, most of which was headed for the nightly campfire.

"They'll probably assume we're headed off to find somewhere private to make out. That's another common element of the classic camp experience. Everybody's nosy about who's having a fling with who."

Why the hell had he said that? Now he was thinking about one of those camp flings and taking it quite a bit further than he ever had as a teenager. Audrey was a beautiful woman, all soft and vulnerable in his arms, and she smelled amazing.

Knock it off, asshole. You've got no business looking at her like that. No business looking at anybody like that.

Audrey had no ready comeback.

"Do you have a lot of trouble with your legs?" Not the greatest segue, but he had to do something to get his mind off the mental images that were making his shorts tighter.

"Only when I've been sitting too long or when I overdo it. Hudson, you really don't have to carry me all the way. Please set me down."

He had a feeling she was minimizing, but he detoured to one of the trail benches and put her down. Because he could still feel her embarrassment, Hudson turned his back, while she wrestled on her socks and shoes.

"Hope you brought some more practical shoes for the rest of the week."

"It was a dance," she argued.

One she'd spent all of with him. Not dancing. But he didn't point that out.

He offered a hand and pulled her to her feet, not asking before he slipped an arm around her. She wobbled a bit but stayed on her feet as they began to walk. Hudson kept his strides short and easy, moving at a pace quicker than the crawl he wanted, to avoid making her feel like an invalid.

"You don't like to take help, do you?"

"If I'd taken all the help people thrust on me after the accident, I'd never have walked again."

"Admitting your limitations doesn't make you weak, Audrey."

She made a little growling noise that was probably meant to convey annoyance but came across as adorable instead. "Screw limitations. I'm here to push past them. I won't know what I can truly do unless I try."

"Which is admirable. But be smart about it. You've got two weeks to ease into things. Don't push yourself so hard you end up benching yourself."

Her gait began to loosen as they went. "You sound like Chad."

Hudson felt a twinge of something. That wasn't jealousy. "Who's Chad? Boyfriend?"

"My physical therapist."

The twinge eased. No, definitely not jealousy. Because that would mean he was interested. Which he definitely was not. He had no business being interested in Audrey Graham, or anyone else for that matter. He was a wreck right now. But he found himself reluctant to let her go once she was able to walk on her own. It felt strangely good to have his arm around her and hers around him.

Where was this desire to look after her coming from? Because he'd rescued her once? He wasn't responsible for her, and he'd more than proved he couldn't look after anybody properly.

He followed her up the cabin steps, watching her feet like a hawk the whole way. But though she moved slowly, her feet didn't hesitate.

She turned on the little porch, tucking a chunk of hair behind one ear. "Thanks for the escort, Hudson. And the conversation."

"No problem." He liked the sound of his name on her lips. Too much.

The moment stretched out between them, feeling strangely date-like, which was absurd. But he couldn't help but wonder what she'd do if he slid a hand into that silky hair and laid his lips over hers. Would they be as soft as they looked? Would her body go pliant against his?

Audrey stepped back, opening the door, and reaching inside to flip on the porch light. "I'll see you tomorrow."

Hudson blinked, shaking himself out of the fantasy. "Tomorrow," he repeated, though he had no idea why. "Good night, Audrey."

"Night."

He waited until she was safely back in her cabin before heading back toward his own. Charlie would undoubtedly be at the campfire, so now was his chance for some quiet time. And maybe he'd manage to fall asleep before his cabinmate got back. Or at least pretend to sleep. Tugging out his phone, he typed a text to his cousin, Rachel. It took ten minutes of hiking before he found enough signal to get it out.

What's the update?

Then he waited.

Three little dots appeared almost immediately. **No change. Get some sleep, Hud.**

Sleep. Right.

Not that he'd done any of that consistently the past few months. Even if he managed to push himself to physical exhaustion, sleep was no reprieve. The moment he closed his eyes, he was back in that goddamned apartment fire. And that was fine. He didn't deserve a reprieve. Didn't deserve to forget, even for a moment. Because that minimized what happened. He'd survived, and he hadn't figured out how to live with that.

As the familiar heaviness set in again, he realized that talking with Audrey was the first time in months he'd felt like himself.

CHAPTER 4

*A*UDREY WOKE TO BIRDSONG.
   Bird song?
   She rolled over, instantly regretting it as her legs screamed. Cracking one eye, she scanned the wooden walls and screen covered windows. Windows that were open to the cool, early morning air. It was a cabin, and she was at camp.

   Sam sat up on the bed across the way, a book propped on her knees, reading glasses sliding down her nose as she looked over at Audrey. "Who is he?"

   "Who's who?" Dear God, she wanted coffee like she wanted her next breath. But coffee was at the lodge, which required walking, which required she do her morning PT so that she could actually use her legs. Damn it.

   "The mystery guy who carried you off last night."

   Hudson.

   Sam set the book aside. "I mean, way to go for getting right on out there. But who is he?"

   "It's not like that." Not in real life anyway. But the snatches of dreams she remembered said otherwise. "I spent too long sitting yesterday, and I was having trouble walking."

Sam's amusement instantly faded. "You okay?"

Audrey covered her eyes with her forearm. "Just embarrassed. Hudson overreacted."

"I saw him carrying you when I was on my way to the camp-fire—we have to go tonight. You're gonna love the s'mores. I thought you were going off to have a romantic tryst."

Audrey flipped the covers back and began to push through the stiffness and pain to stretch and loosen up her muscles.

He'd said people would make that assumption. But more in a matter-of-fact sort of way than in an I'd-be-into-that tone. Not that her dreams had gotten the message. In that version, he'd kissed her goodnight, taking her mouth with the same unhesi-tating confidence with which he'd scooped her up to carry her back. Even the memory of that dream kiss had heat crawling up her cheeks.

"Sadly, no."

"It's early in camp yet. There's time. I mean, there's obviously interest there since you two sat outside and talked for *two hours*."

If the party hadn't broken up, would they have talked more? Audrey felt like she could've talked with him all night. When was the last time she'd met anyone interesting enough for that?

She pulled one leg into her chest, straightening her knee and pointing her toe toward the ceiling. "It's not that simple. We have a sort of history."

"Oh really?" Sam drew the word out to four syllables. "How does one have a 'sort of history'?"

Audrey readjusted and held the stretch, breathing through the pain until the cramp in her calf released. "He's the firefighter who cut me out of my car."

"Seriously?"

"Yeah." Her own, personal hero.

"How does that even come up in conversation? I thought you didn't remember much from the accident."

"I don't. But I remembered his voice. It's a great voice. Sort of deep and rumbly, like the purr of a giant cat."

Sam pursed her lips.

Audrey felt her cheeks heat. "Don't look at me like that."

"Like what?"

"Like it's a weird thing to fixate on."

"I didn't say a thing."

"That voice kept me sane and grounded, when there was a very good chance I was dying. It stuck with me."

Sam sobered. "Well, I think the fact that he's here, now, is a thing. Sounds like fate to me."

Now it was Audrey's turn to give her the side eye. "There's no such thing as fate."

"You don't think it's weird that you're both here?"

"He's the one who told me about this place. He talked about it while he was cutting me out. I remembered. That's it."

"So, really, you came here because of him."

Had he been somewhere in the back of her mind when she'd discovered Camp Firefly Falls was an option? Maybe. "I suppose, in a roundabout kind of way, yes. But that's not fate. It's just… logical consequence."

"Logical consequence. God, you're such a scientist."

"We didn't all get our PhDs by analyzing the literary ravings of dead white dudes."

"Dead white *women*, thank you very much. So you, from your vaunted, rational science position, are saying you didn't dig the hot firefighter?"

"I never said he was hot."

"So, he's not?"

"No, he's smoking." The words slipped out before Audrey could think better of them. But why not? Sam would see for herself it was true at some point.

"I rest my case. Look, you came here to make up for all those experiences you didn't have before the accident. A time-honored tradition is the summer camp fling. He seems like an excellent candidate."

Audrey had no desire to analyze the way her heart jumped at that idea. Sure, she was here to push outside her comfort zone, but deliberately pursuing a guy? She couldn't imagine doing something like that. She was too awkward, too cerebral, too... something. Ignoring the faint whisper of *Chicken* in the back of her mind, she turned the conversation back on her friend. "Did you have a camp fling?"

"My first kiss was at camp." Sam's face took on a dreamy expression as she wrapped her arms around her pillow in a hug. "Jordan Marshall on the last night of camp, when I was thirteen. It was terribly romantic."

First kiss at thirteen? Audrey had been a senior in college before she'd crossed that bridge. And when the other senior she'd gone out with had found out she was about to graduate at nineteen at the top of their class, he'd suddenly gotten very busy pretending she didn't exist. She didn't want to think about Cas the Ass.

"So, what happened to Jordan?"

"No idea. He never came back to camp. At least not while I was there. We just had the one kiss. Helluva kiss though." She shifted her focus back to Audrey. "I want that for you. A helluva kiss. A superior make out session. Hell, a flaming hot affair. You deserve to live as much as you want while you're here. Whether that's with your firefighter or with somebody else."

Her firefighter. Audrey shouldn't like the sound of that so much. Hudson wasn't her firefighter. Her hero, yes. Whether he wanted to admit it or not. But definitely not hers in any real sense of the word.

Did she want to change that? And if she did, did she have the guts to try?

Audrey didn't know. Beyond their unusual circumstantial connection, he intrigued her. More, he'd treated her like a normal woman, not a freaktastic brainiac. Not as damaged. Even when accommodating her condition because of her injuries, she hadn't felt like he thought she was broken. So, yeah. Fling-bait or not, she wanted to get to know him better. But that meant she had to find him first.

Physical therapy exercises complete, Audrey stood and reached for some jeans. "Right now, the only relationship I'm interested in is the one with my coffee cup. Let's go get breakfast."

DESPITE THE HUNDRED or so other people wandering the grounds, Hudson managed to spend the day completely alone out on the water. He'd kayaked the full length of the lake, well past the bounds of Camp Firefly Falls property. He'd seen others out on the water but hadn't come close enough to speak to any of them. He'd even found a hidden cove to beach the kayak and string up his portable hammock for an afternoon nap. It had been nice not having any of his friends or family checking up on him, trying to poke without looking like they were poking, to see how he was. He'd forgotten how peaceful it was up here.

But he'd found himself thinking about Audrey off and on all day, wondering how she was getting on with her first day of camp. He hadn't seen her. In the privacy of his own head, he could admit he'd been looking. He hoped she hadn't suffered any lasting ill effects from whatever was going on with her legs, and that she could get out and enjoy herself the way she wanted. He told himself it was a craving for s'mores that drove him to the nightly campfire, not that he was seeking her out. The little bump of pleasure under his breastbone as he saw her sitting to one side of the fire made him a liar.

She was in animated conversation with some other campers. "It was *awesome!*"

He had no idea what was awesome, but the delight in her voice made his lips curve. Good. She deserved to have a good time and check some more stuff off the life list she'd told him about last night. He didn't interrupt her conversation, instead heading for the s'mores supplies. She caught his eye as he dipped a hand into the bag of marshmallows, sending him a sunny wave before going back to her conversation. Sliding a couple of marshmallows onto his stick, he settled on the opposite side of the fire, where he could covertly watch her as she smoothly rotated her own marshmallows above the flames.

She was so... Bright was the word that kept coming to mind. Even with the hesitation he'd noticed last night, she was so thirsty for new experiences, showing a level of enthusiasm for totally basic things that most people took for granted. Who got that excited about paddle boating? It was something he'd always found dull, but listening to her talk about her afternoon on the lake, he couldn't help but smile.

"Okay, marshmallow toasting perfection achieved. There is no way to top that."

"Of course, there is. With chocolate and another graham cracker." Another woman held some out and sandwiched the marshmallow goo between them.

Audrey took the treat with careful hands and bit in, her eyes going comically wide as she started fanning with one hand. *"Hot!"*

Her friend laughed. "You're supposed to wait a little bit for it to cool off. Here, have some water."

Audrey washed it down, then almost immediately took another bite. "I didn't need the skin on the roof of my mouth anyway. Holy crap, this is so much better over a real fire."

"Told ya," her friend said, smug.

Audrey polished off the s'more with a happy little moan that had parts of him thinking happy thoughts as well. His stick dipped and his marshmallow caught fire.

"Shit." Hudson yanked it back and blew out the flame.

Eyes twinkling, Audrey stood up and stepped forward, extending her hands to warm them. "Need a refresher?"

"Some people like them charred." He wasn't one of them, but she didn't need to know that. He popped the blackened lump of sugar into his mouth and chewed. "Good day?"

Her smile spread wide. The sight of it did funny things to his chest.

"Great day. I made pottery."

"Enjoyed getting your hands dirty, huh?"

"So much." She laughed. Someone called her name and she turned.

Everything seemed to snap into slow motion. Hudson could see her pivot, see her knee buckling, her balance failing, tipping her toward the heart of the fire.

He didn't hesitate. He exploded up, leaping through the flames. With relief, he felt the impact of her body against his, their combined momentum carrying her away from certain disaster. He twisted, wrapping himself around her so that it was him who hit the ground first, cushioning her landing.

For an instant, he froze, his body remembering the fall as the roof gave way. Phantom flames licked him from all sides, and he could see Steve falling beside him, slamming into a railing, and plummeting down the stairwell.

Not real. Not now. Audrey.

Hudson shoved himself up, running his hands over her, checking for flames, for burns. Frantic. A dim, distant part of himself recognized he was kind of losing his shit. Which was the reason he hadn't been out on any fire calls in three months. He couldn't be trusted to hold it together.

Soft, cool hands pressed against his cheeks. "Hudson, I'm okay."

His brain short circuited, abruptly cutting off the panic.

Audrey was sprawled across his lap. As he focused on her face, she gave him a lopsided smile. "Well, I guess you can take the fireman out of the turnout pants."

God, yes.

It was clearly meant to be a joke, but his dick didn't get the message. It leapt to attention, ready and willing to burn through some of the adrenaline still pumping through his system.

He saw the moment she caught the sexual undertone. Those bright blue eyes went dark, and the pulse at the base of her throat began to throb.

And they were surrounded by at least a dozen other people.

"Dude, that was amazing."

"Are you *insane?*"

"No, he's a firefighter."

"Are *you* burned?" Audrey asked.

Would he even register if he were? "No." If he found anything later, he knew well enough how to deal with it.

They disentangled themselves. Hudson rolled to his feet and reached down to pull Audrey to hers. She wobbled a little but stood on her own, no apparent lingering issues in her legs.

"Why don't you walk me back?"

Which was how Hudson found himself on the trail, alone with Audrey a few minutes later. He was mortified to realize he was shaking. The adrenaline dump was a killer.

Once they were out of earshot, she touched his arm. "Are you okay?"

No, no he was definitely not okay. He hadn't been okay for three months. But he wasn't gonna talk about that.

"You're really okay?" he asked instead.

"I really am, thanks to you. Again." Her face twisted with chagrin. "I swear, I'm not normally that much of a klutz."

She'd nearly fallen into a campfire from nothing more than turning wrong. His heart still hadn't quite settled back to normal. He could too easily imagine the damage if he hadn't caught her in time. The woman needed a keeper.

They arrived back at her cabin, and he found himself in the exact same position he'd been in last night. Because he wanted to touch her, Hudson shoved his hands in his pockets.

Audrey turned toward him with a sweet smile. "Thanks for walking me back."

"Sure." Hudson wanted to maybe thank her for getting him the hell away from all those people before he made more of a fool of himself. But that would require admitting it had happened, and he wasn't doing that either.

She lingered, tucking a chunk of hair behind her ear. Her tongue darted out to moisten her lips.

She's waiting for me to kiss her. The realization slammed into him. He wanted to. And it wasn't just because of the lingering adrenaline buzz. He'd been thinking about it since last night, wondering if her hair was as silky soft as it looked and if she'd be hesitant or if she'd throw herself into a kiss with the same kind of enthusiasm she'd shown for everything else at camp. Which was stupid. He didn't know this woman. Not really. She'd come up here to have some fun and accomplish some stuff on her bucket list. The last thing she needed was to get dragged down by all his shit.

Hudson took a step back. "Glad you're okay." He ignored the way her face fell a little and told himself he was doing them both a favor. "See you around, Audrey."

Before he could change his mind, he turned away and disappeared into the darkness, her soft "Good night" lingering in his ears.

CHAPTER 5

"SOMEBODY'S GOT A CAMP crush."

Audrey looked up as Charlie sat down at their table, a plate piled high with bacon and eggs in his hands. "What?"

"Hudson, sugar. He's talking about Hudson," Sam clarified.

Did they mean he had a crush on *her?* Surely, they meant the reverse, which—okay, yeah, she kinda did have a camp crush on Hudson. Not that it mattered.

"The guy *jumped through a fire* to keep you from falling into it last night. I hope you rewarded him appropriately for his heroics," Charlie continued.

Sam picked up her coffee. "I had two extra s'mores to give you time in case you did."

Audrey's cheeks burned as she remembered the look in his eyes. Even she'd recognized the expression of absolute hunger. If there hadn't been all those people around maybe there might've been...something.

"He walked me back to the cabin like a gentleman. There was no hanky panky, so your caloric sacrifice was for nothing."

"Opportunity lost." Charlie paused. "Unless you're with somebody back home and not free."

"She's available," Sam informed him.

"Then I stick to my original assessment. He at least deserved a kiss."

She'd been willing. But there'd been more than simple attraction and adrenaline-fueled arousal going on last night. She'd lain awake a long time thinking about it, about him. There'd been something in his eyes, in the frenetic movement of his hands as he'd checked her for injury. As if, for just a little while, it hadn't been her he was seeing.

She understood those moments of being not quite connected to the present because something from the past still had a hold. For the most part, she'd moved past the nightmares and the flashbacks, but she recognized someone still suffering. It made her want to be Hudson's friend. To earn his trust, learn his issues, and find a way to help him deal. And that was a very different thing from the uncomplicated camp fling her friends were imagining.

"I'm starting to see why you're a romance editor," Audrey said.

"I love love," he declared. "And it makes me a total hit with the ladies."

"Be that as it may, I'm pretty sure he's not here looking for anything of the sort."

"Don't you read? All the best relationships happen when you're not looking," Sam insisted.

Audrey sipped her coffee and decided their brains had been addled by spending too much time in fiction and not enough in real life. Or maybe not. What did she know? It wasn't like she was an example of "normal" in any category.

She opened her mouth to change the subject but trailed off as she saw Hudson walk in. Surely it was a crime in several states to look that hot in basketball shorts and a t-shirt. He moved with an easy grace and economy of motion that she appreciated on a whole different level since walking had become a thing she had to actively think about so as not to face plant on a regular basis.

Charlie let out a whistle and waved Hudson over. His gaze

skimmed over them, lingering for a moment on her before he lifted his hand in a wave and began loading his plate from the continental breakfast. Audrey didn't think he'd join them, but a few minutes later, he was pulling out the chair beside her and dropping into it.

"Morning." Since when did she sound like a teenage girl, all breathless and excited?

Hudson grunted and shoved bacon into his mouth.

Okay then. Not a morning person.

Audrey searched his face for lingering signs of...whatever she thought she'd seen last night, but he was relaxed and focused on his breakfast. He'd shaved and his hair was damp from a shower or swim. Because she wanted to stare—he was a fine thing to see first thing in the morning—she clutched her coffee like a shield and changed the subject. "What's on today's activities list? I didn't look before we left the cabin."

"Didn't you hear? It's Field Day," Charlie replied.

"Field Day?"

"Yeah! It's a full day of relay races, water games, target games, tug of war. It's awesome."

It didn't sound awesome to Audrey. It sounded like torture. She was aware of Hudson's gaze on her as Charlie continued.

"They'll probably have us pair up or divide into teams."

Teams. Meaning competitions. Meaning winners and losers. Anybody paired with her would automatically come in dead last. She couldn't run anymore and wasn't coordinated enough to do anything fast. She was a liability to any kind of competition. Maybe some of the other activities would still be open. She could hide out in the pottery studio and play so Sam wouldn't feel obligated to partner up with her.

"Winner gets to pick the movie tonight. I heard they were setting up a projector on the side of the lodge," Sam said. "Obviously, we'll be together for girl power."

Audrey opened her mouth to make an excuse, but before she could get it out, Hudson spoke up.

"She already promised to be my partner." He shifted calm gray eyes to hers. "Remember?"

She had, of course, done no such thing. He'd barely said a dozen words since they left the campfire last night. Snapping her mouth closed, she looked at him, trying to figure out if he was messing with her. He just stared back, placid as could be, and took a bite of toast.

"Well you should definitely go with Hudson. Charlie?" Sam asked.

"All yours, sweetness." He shoved back from the chair. "Shall we go plot strategy?"

Sam wasn't actually finished with her breakfast, but she shoved the last couple of slices of bacon onto her bagel and rose. "Let's. We'll see y'all on the field!"

Like rats jumping from a sinking ship. That was fine. She didn't much want to have this conversation with an audience.

Audrey waited until they left to speak. "You don't have to do this. I can go do something else."

"Do you *want* to do something else?"

No. Damn it. She wanted to be included. She'd never been included as a kid because nobody wanted the baby on their team. But she didn't want to be the pity pick, even if it was by her camp crush. Maybe especially by her camp crush. "You'll end up losing with me as a partner."

"I'm not in it to win. I'm in it so you can be."

She hadn't known him long, but she felt confident that spending the day surrounded by dozens of other rowdy campers was not what he really wanted to be doing. He'd come up here for solitude. "Why?"

"Because you deserve a shot at the authentic camp experience. This is part of it. And...because it's fun for me to see you get excited about all this stuff." He shrugged those massive shoulders as if uncomfortable with the admission.

"Excited is a strong word. I'm not sure I can physically *do* a lot of this stuff. I mean, maybe if I had no time clock and no audience, but..." She trailed off, too able to imagine falling on her butt in front of all of camp. Not that falling on her ass was a new experience since the accident. But there'd already been half a dozen people by their table this morning to ask if she was okay after the fire last night. She didn't relish any other entries that confirmed her position as camp klutz, and she wasn't keen on advertising the reason why. She didn't want to become the entire camp's object of pity.

"Do you trust me?" He'd leaned forward when she wasn't paying attention, so the rumble of his voice came near to her ear. Why should just the sound of it continue to soothe her anxieties?

"What does that have to do with anything?"

"It's a simple question. Do you?"

She had a simple and instinctive answer. "Yes." With her life, certainly. Though bringing that up right now seemed like overkill.

"Then meet me at the soccer fields at ten. And bring your game face."

"WELCOME TO FIELD DAY, CAMPERS!" Heather's voice boomed from the bull horn from where she stood in the center of the soccer fields. "Everybody have their partner?"

A cheer went up from the assembled crowd. Well, everybody but Audrey. She stood beside Hudson, arms crossed over the number nine pinned to her shirt, mouth set in a grim line. He was starting to wonder whether pushing her into this was such a good idea. But he'd seen the expression of half longing, half regret in her sky-blue eyes when Charlie brought Field Day up, and he'd hated it. It was such a departure from the fierce determination she'd shown the other night when she'd talked about pushing her limits. So, he'd made the snap decision to be her partner and help her through the stuff she found physically difficult. He didn't think they'd win, but he figured he could keep her from coming in last place.

"We're kicking things off today with a camp classic. The wheelbarrow race. One partner will be the wheelbarrow, the other will hold that person by the legs and push. The object is to get all the way down to the orange cones, circle around, and make it back to the starting line as fast as you can. Partners, take your positions!"

Audrey took a slow breath and let it back out. "Obviously, I'm the wheelbarrow."

"Ever done this before?"

She lifted a brow in his direction. "What do you think?"

Okay, yeah. She wasn't excited about this *at all.*

Hudson caught her arm as she headed for the starting line. "We can walk away right now."

Those eyes licked with temper. "I'm no quitter."

The faint tone of insult had him smiling. "That's my girl. Let's go."

At the starting line, she looked at the other players getting in position and dropped down to all fours.

"The key to this is keeping your core tight and focusing on one step at a time with your hands. Don't think about anybody else," he told her.

"Got it."

"On your marks!" Heather called.

Audrey rose into a push-up, and Hudson couldn't help but notice the flex of muscle in her shoulders and arms beneath the tank top she wore.

"Get set!"

He grasped her by the ankles and lifted.

"Go!"

She took off, all but running on her hands. They edged to the front of the pack, neck-and-neck with two other teams. He kept a close eye on her, expecting her to start flagging any second. The team to their left went down in a heap. Curses rose on the air, but Audrey kept moving, smooth and steady as they neared the cone. The team ahead on the right fell over into a pile of giggles as they rounded their cone. Audrey didn't fumble once as they entered the final stretch and took the lead.

"We've got this," he said. "Just keep doing what you're doing."

In his periphery, Hudson saw a couple of guys closing in, the wheelbarrow guy eating up the distance with his longer arms. Audrey saw him too. Was she *growling*? Hell yes, she was.

"Push!" she shouted.

So, he did. She threw her arms out, reaching, bucking, until she was practically galloping on her hands.

"Almost there!" he yelled.

Audrey leapt for the finish line, tucking into a graceless somersault as they crossed to a shout of "Tie!"

Hudson squatted down beside her. "That was awesome! You were a beast."

From where she lay sprawled, panting on the ground, she peered up at him. "Wheelchairs are great for developing upper body strength and coordination."

He wondered how long she'd spent in one over the last couple of years but wasn't about to ask. Instead, he offered a hand and tugged her into a sitting position. "Ready to go kick some more ass?"

She turned to glare at their competition and narrowed her eyes to slits. "It is *on!* Help me up."

After her reluctance to even admit she needed help the other night, this felt like a different kind of victory. She wrapped her hands around his forearms and he rose, lifting them both to their feet. Audrey wobbled a bit, stumbling into him. Instinctively, he shifted to steady her, one hand going to her waist and brushing bare skin where her shirt had ridden up. Before he could stop himself, he rubbed a thumb along the smooth warmth of her flesh. Her fingers tightened on his arms, her pupils blowing wide. It would be so easy to slide his hand around to the small of her back and pull her against him—

"Good job everybody!" Heather's voice rang out over the cheers of the crowd. "Big round of applause for Team 4 and Team 9, who are currently tied for first place."

Hudson let her go before he could give in to the terrible idea that kept kicking around in his head, barely noticing the back thumps and fist bumps of congratulations. He was here for Audrey. But he wasn't here *for* Audrey. It was best he remember that.

If any hint of arousal lingered, she hid it well, throwing herself into the next round of activity. And that was just fine. It helped him keep his head in the games. Whatever trepidation she'd felt at the prospect of participating seemed to have evaporated. They lost their lead in the sack race. No surprise, and Hudson was grateful Audrey didn't hurt herself. The impact of all that jumping had to be rough on her knees. Not that she uttered a word of complaint. They made up for lost points in the bean bag toss. Turned out she had wicked good aim. With Hudson edging out the competition in the football toss, they were just clinging to third place as they prepared for the three-legged race.

"Which is your dominant leg?" he asked.

"Used to be left. These days it doesn't really matter." She tipped back a bottle of water and guzzled it.

Hudson moved around to her right side and bent to tie their legs together at the ankles. Audrey was shaking as Hudson straightened. "You okay?"

"Tired. I'm not used to exerting myself quite this much." Her cheeks were flushed and wisps of hair clung to her damp face, but she didn't seem to be in pain.

He slid an arm around her, as much out of a desire to comfort as to keep his balance. "We just need to get through this last event, then we break for lunch."

"I never dreamed we'd be in this long." She finished off the water and glanced up at him through lowered lashes. "Looks like we make a good team."

"Looks like."

It was too easy to imagine her words meant more. Because they did make a good team. She was easy to be with. No pressure, no worries—well, other than keeping an eye out for her general safety. Their silences were comfortable. Yeah, if he were looking for a camp fling, Audrey Graham would absolutely be it.

"Teams, take your positions!" Heather called.

Audrey slid her arm around his waist. "Ready to annihilate the competition?"

Hudson found himself grinning. "I like the way you think."

CHAPTER 6

*T*HEY DIDN'T WIN.

EVEN with Hudson practically carrying her during the three-legged race, they came in fourth. They slid further in the rankings in the water balloon toss, and things sort of went downhill from there. Audrey didn't care. She not only got to participate, but she and Hudson finished a respectable sixth out of twenty teams. They'd had *fun.* Then she'd promptly headed back to her cabin, taken a scalding shower in an effort to beat her muscles loose, and passed out. She'd slept through dinner. Maybe there'd be popcorn at the movie. She wondered what the winners had picked for everybody to watch.

Halfway to the lodge, she realized she should've put on more layers. The concept of long sleeves in June for anything other than blocking the sun simply did not compute. But she was already late for the start of the movie, and her stomach was making a bid to devour itself. They'd set up a screen on the side of the main lodge. An older Kurt Russell, dressed in clothes that should've stayed in the eighties, sat at a bar, eating nachos. She didn't recognize the movie, which meant it probably didn't fall into the category of funny or romantic flicks she preferred. Campers spread out on the lawn in canvas chairs or lounging on blankets. Several had popcorn and adult beverages. Hallelujah. Skirting the edge of the crowd, she looked for Sam and the source of the snacks.

"Audrey."

Following the sound of the low voice, she saw Hudson occupying a blanket a few rows from the back. He waved her over. Trying not to block people's views too much, she picked her way to him and lowered herself to the blanket beside him.

"Thought you were gonna be a no show," he whispered.

It gave her a warm glow that he'd been looking for her. She didn't know exactly what they were doing, but there'd been enough moments and long looks that she was certain he wasn't indifferent to her. Which wasn't the same thing as being into her, but she'd take it for a win.

"Overslept." Her stomach felt compelled to punctuate the statement.

"Missed dinner. Twizzler?" He offered her the open pack.

Well, it wasn't popcorn, but it was something. She plucked a couple of red ropes out and bit in, nodding toward the screen. "What is this?"

"Some Quentin Tarantino crap. *Death Proof.* Never seen it, but one of the guys at my fire house raved about it. Can't remember what it's about. So far it's pretty terrible."

Conscious of the other campers, she kept her voice quiet. "Aren't most Tarantino films all about drugs, violence, and spectacle?"

"Seems like," he conceded. "I figure some kind of explosion is imminent."

"What would you have picked if we'd won?"

"*Die Hard.* Or maybe *Jaws.*"

Audrey nodded and started on the second Twizzler. "Classics."

"What about you?"

"Well, at a place like this, it seems only fitting to pick *Dirty Dancing.*"

He made a show of rolling his eyes and groaning softly. "My sister loves that movie."

"Every girl loves that movie. Or at the very least loves Patrick Swayze's very fine backside."

"Did you have the whole lift fantasy?"

She laughed. "No. And Sam won't watch it with me because I'm too apt to point out that there's no way Baby and Johnny make it. She goes off to the Peace Corps and does amazing things with her life."

"What about him?"

"I think he dances as long as he can and then, when the world changes, he probably ends up in some kind of trade job. Construction, maybe. But he never forgot the girl who stood up for him in the face of prejudice."

"Not a romantic?"

Audrey started to stretch out, then changed her mind as a sudden gust of wind had gooseflesh rising on her arms. "I like romance as much as the next girl. I just don't look for it in real life or expect it to have a permanent happy ending."

He shrugged out of his hoodie and wrapped it around her shoulders.

"How gallant. Thank you." She slid her arms into the sleeves and zipped it up, just barely resisting the urge to drop her nose to the fabric to inhale his scent.

"So, you're a cynic."

"Realist. Happily ever after is an unrealistic fantasy. Life happens. People talk about happiness as if it's this static state of being, and that's wrong. Happiness is a mindset, no matter what's going on in your life. It's a continual choice."

When she shivered again, Hudson wrapped his arm around her and tucked her against his side. It hadn't been a calculated move on her part, but she wasn't about to complain. After only a moment's hesitation, she burrowed in.

"Is that why you're so happy?"

Right now, she was happy to be sharing body heat. "I suppose so. Research shows that people who willfully choose to be positive about their situation in life have better outcomes than those who focus on the negative. I figured I needed every advantage I could give myself during my recovery." She shrugged. "I guess the attitude stuck."

He turned his head toward hers. "I like the attitude."

Only a couple of inches separated their mouths. Audrey wondered what he'd do if she tipped her face to close the distance. Did she really have the nerve to do it?

On the screen, some woman was getting into Kurt Russell's muscle car.

Something shifted in Hudson's face. "Let's get out of here."

Her pulse leapt. She was inclined to follow him anywhere, so she nodded. But there was a strange urgency to him as he pulled her up and into motion, wrapping an arm around her.

"Let's go."

Laughing softly, she did her best to keep up. "What's the hurry?"

"We need to go." The deadly serious tone was entirely at odds with the little fantasy playing out in her head of being hauled away to make out.

"Why?"

"Because I just remembered why Rodney was raving about this movie and you really don't need to see it."

Behind them, Audrey could hear an engine and squealing tires. She stumbled.

Hudson's arm tightened around her. "Just keep walking. Whatever you do, don't look." His voice thrummed with command.

They'd rounded the corner of the lodge when the crash came —a horrific rending of metal that seemed to go on repeating long after it should've been over, echoing off the nearby buildings. The sound reached into her and twisted, ripping open memories best left to darkness. Her body whipped with the shock of impact. There was one, long, surreal moment of weightlessness before the second hit came and her world narrowed down to nothing but stunning, unspeakable pain, as her car crumpled around her.

HUDSON BARELY KEPT Audrey from hitting the ground as she dropped like a stone.

"Audrey? Audrey!"

Her face had gone ashen. The pulse in her throat thundered way too fast and her breathing was ragged. She wasn't unconscious, but she wasn't with him either.

Shit, shit, shit. Why hadn't he realized and gotten her out of there sooner?

He scooped her up, tucking her close against his chest as he tried to figure out where to take her. His cabin? Hers? Too far, he decided. What was close? He scanned the buildings, wondering what was unlocked.

The kitchen.

"Stay with me, baby." Remembering she'd said the sound of his voice had helped after the accident, he kept up a running monologue as he made a beeline across the grassy space, circling around until he found a door. Unlocked, thank God. It opened under his hand and he pushed into the dark space. The faint glow of the emergency Exit sign lit the entryway. He turned into the kitchen proper and found an empty room full of gleaming stainless steel.

With nowhere else to go, Hudson sank down to the floor, his back pressed to one of the long counters. Audrey's small body quaked against him. He stroked her hair and curled around her. Talking. Talking. "It's okay. It's over. I've got you. Come back to the now, Audrey."

"Hurts," she gasped.

"I know. But you survived it. You came out the other side. Where are you now?"

Her teeth chattered through the shock. "Camp."

"That's right. Camp Firefly Falls in the Berkshires." Hudson wished he had a blanket to wrap her in. "Do you know who you're with?"

Audrey turned her face into his throat, a child-like motion that absolutely undid him. "My hero."

His heart pinched. He didn't deserve that title. Not really. Any of his crew could have been the one to cut her out of that car. And nothing he'd done since they got here was heroic. But if thinking that helped pull her out of the grip of the flashback, he wasn't going to argue.

At length, her shaking stopped and her breath evened out. He wondered if she'd fallen asleep.

"Thank you."

Apparently not. "For what?"

"For getting me away."

Another wave of self-recriminations crashed over him. "Not fast enough."

"Believe me, it would've been worse if I'd seen it."

"I'm sorry. I should've realized sooner."

"We both should've used the brains God gave us and walked away when we found out it was Tarantino. Enough said." She lifted her head. "Thank you for taking care of me. I don't think Sam was out there, and I really don't want to think about everybody in camp being privy to me having a panic attack."

Hudson couldn't stop himself from tucking a lock of loose hair behind her ear. Taking care of her was as natural as breathing. He didn't really want to analyze why that was the case. "Still hurting?"

"It's fading. I'll be okay in a little while."

"Think an ice cream sundae might help?"

She let loose a little bubble of surprised laughter. "What?"

"Well, you never did get dinner, and we're in the kitchen.

Might as well make a raid." Maybe he could turn this night around and take her mind off what had just happened. "Middle of the night kitchen raids are a camp tradition."

"Think they still stock the same staples they had when you were a kid?"

"If there isn't an industrial size vat of peanut butter and an equally large container of vanilla ice cream, I'll be most disappointed."

Her lips curved, some of the strain leaving her face. "Let's find out."

They disentangled themselves and got to their feet. Audrey used the counters for balance as she made her way to the doorway. Hudson itched to set her on one of them so he could do all the work, but maybe it was good for her to move. She reached for a light switch.

"Stop! Lights off for a kitchen raid." He dug out his phone and switched on the flashlight app.

"Hey! That's contraband. We're supposed to be cell phone free these two weeks."

"I'm a rebel." He didn't want to get into his reasons for keeping his phone. Moving over to join her, they made their way to the commercial freezer and tugged it open. "Bingo." Hudson hauled out the giant tub of vanilla ice cream.

"I'll check the fridge for toppings." She opened the next door and ducked her head inside, while he searched the shelves pantry.

Ten minutes later, they'd turned up all the fixings for ice cream sundaes.

"One scoop or two?" he asked.

"Three. No dinner, remember?"

"A woman after my own heart." Hudson scooped three blobs of ice cream into bowls for each of them.

Audrey followed with chocolate syrup, peanut butter, and whipped cream. She topped them off with chopped pecans. "Cherry?"

"I do not like fruit with my ice cream."

"It's not my favorite, but I feel like sundaes are a personal challenge to try to tie the cherry stem into a knot with my tongue." She bit the cherry off and popped the stem into her mouth.

"Ever managed it?"

Holding up a finger, she worked her mouth, face twisted in fierce concentration. Amused, he picked up his sundae and spooned up a bite as he watched. A couple of minutes later, she opened her mouth and plucked out a knotted cherry stem.

The thought of how agile her tongue had to be to pull that off had his brain veering back into dangerous territory. He was grateful for the relative darkness as he gave a slow clap. "I'm impressed."

Audrey boosted herself up onto the counter and picked up her own sundae, digging in with gusto. "God. This is so good."

"Middle of the night ice cream usually is."

"I'm glad you thought of it. And I'm glad you're a nice enough guy to be trying to pretend you aren't doomed to see me at my worst."

"I don't always see you at your worst."

"That's not *all* you've seen," she conceded. "But you met me when I was broken and on the verge of dying. You rescued me from falling into a fire because of my own klutziness. And you've just masterfully handled a total flashback to the accident. I have not managed to present my best face with you."

"I like your face." The words were out before he could think better of them. But what the hell? It was true. "And there's no shame in any of those things. The accident wasn't your fault. The fact that your legs don't always cooperate isn't your fault—and, the fact that they cooperate at all is a testament to how much you've busted your ass. And I know exactly what it's like to be dragged into memories of the worst day of your life." Damn it. He hadn't meant to say that either. She was too easy to talk to.

"For what it's worth, I like your face, too."

She wasn't going to ask. Something in his chest unclenched at that realization, and he found himself smiling.

Hudson scooped up more ice cream. "So, what's on the docket tomorrow?"

"I was thinking maybe ziplining. I always wanted to go, and the system they have set up here is supposed to be pretty awesome."

"You up to that after today?"

"I think so. The pain and stiffness are worse if I stop moving."

"Okay then. I'll meet you there after breakfast."

Audrey angled her head, studying him in that intent way she had. "Why?"

Because he liked her. Because he wanted to keep her safe, so she could enjoy her time here at camp. And because when he was with her, he didn't feel quite so shitty about himself. But he didn't say any of that. "Because I haven't been ziplining in nearly twenty years, and it sounds like fun."

She smiled another one of those sunrise smiles that made his chest go tight. "Okay then. See you after breakfast."

CHAPTER 7

"SOOOO, YOU AND HUDSON disappeared awfully fast from the movie last night," Sam observed.

And then I promptly lost my shit. But Audrey wasn't about to talk about that. The more mental distance she could put between herself and last night's flashback, the better. "It's not what you think. We just decided to do a kitchen raid since I slept through dinner. The movie was shitty anyway."

"You should've come and joined us for poker in the boathouse," Charlie said.

"Next time."

Sam narrowed her eyes. "You okay? You seem a little peaked this morning."

"Fine. Just tired. Didn't sleep well. There's a reason our moms wouldn't let us have giant ice cream sundaes for dinner right before bed." *Right. Let's blame it on the sugar.*

"If ice cream is the only thing you topped with whipped cream last night, then you and Hud need lessons in how this whole fling thing is supposed to work," Charlie announced.

"We're not having a fling." And after last night, the likelihood that they ever would seemed minuscule. Was she doomed to always show her absolute worst to this man?

"That's a damned shame. You two throw off sparks every time you get within ten feet of each other," Sam observed.

Yeah. Yeah it was. Tired of the discussion, Audrey drained the last of her coffee and shoved back from the table. "Well, at the risk of encouraging your romantic delusions, I'm bidding you both good day. I'm meeting Hudson at the zipline this morning."

"Oooo," they chorused.

Audrey rolled her eyes, hearing a faint sing-song of "Audrey and Hudson sitting in a tree…" as she pushed out of the dining hall. She couldn't decide if she was annoyed or amused.

He was waiting at the head of the zipline trail, dressed in cargo shorts and a navy SFD t-shirt. The stretch of cotton across his broad shoulders had her mouth watering. Just the sight of him had last night's horror fading.

His lips quirked in a half-smile as he saw her. "Morning."

That voice. Dear God. There was an extra layer of growl to the rumble this morning, and added to the stubble darkening his jaw, she couldn't help but think about what it'd be like to hear that voice in bed, maybe with that stubble rubbing against more sensitive parts.

Audrey slammed the door on that thought and sucked in an unnecessarily large lungful of crisp, morning air. "Hi." *Brilliant conversationalist, Graham. How dare he not throw himself directly at your feet?*

"You ready for this?"

For just a moment, she forgot what she was here for. Was she ready to say to hell with caution and pursue him? Her brain said hell no. Her lady parts were screaming, "Move over sister!" Then she remembered. Ziplining. They were here to go flying through trees together.

"As I'll ever be." Even she didn't know which question she was answering.

"Scared?"

Terrified. "Maybe a little nervous."

He smiled like he knew she was lying and gestured to the trail. "After you."

A part of her wanted to slip her hand into his, like a giddy teenager on a first date. Instead she started walking.

He fell into step beside her. "Nothing to worry about. You'll be strapped into a safety harness the whole time. You don't even have to hold on."

Oh, but she wanted to hold on. To him.

What is the matter with me? She'd never in her life had a conversation where everything sounded like a double-entendre. Never had a conversation where she couldn't keep her mind off sex. She'd had sex and hadn't been all that impressed with it, so the lack of it since the accident hadn't even really registered. Not until now.

He's an excellent specimen of a man. Big. Muscular. Virile. And you've got a little hero worship going on. Why wouldn't you? He's done nothing but repeatedly rescue you since you met. You're just a slave to biology. That's all. It means you're a healthy, adult female. That should be a comfort.

It wasn't.

"Audrey?"

She realized they'd stopped at a little gear hut, and Hudson had been talking to her. "Hmm?"

"You okay?"

"Woolgathering. I'm sorry. You were saying?"

He held out a bright red helmet. "Try this one on for size."

She put it on. With expert fingers, he checked the fit, snapping and adjusting straps until the thing fit properly. "You do this a lot?"

"Ziplining, no. But rock climbing, yes. And search and rescue training. A lot of the equipment is very similar. Here, let's get you harnessed up." He accepted a harness from the girl manning the hut and bent low, holding it out so Audrey could step into it. "Just put your legs through here."

She balanced on his shoulder and put one foot through, then the other, proud she didn't wobble. She'd done extra stretches this morning to make sure she was as limber as possible. As thrilling as his rescue had been the other night, the realities of her continued limitations and klutziness made her paranoid about the necessity for a repeat. "I thought you were part of a city fire department."

"I am. But I'm certified for search and rescue. Sometimes I get called out for work elsewhere." He pulled the harness up to her hips and started adjusting those straps.

Audrey tried not to think too much about the proximity of his hands as they tightened and tugged, jerking her hips around a bit as he worked.

"All set. You wanna check my work?"

The staff woman nodded and looked Audrey over while Hudson put on his own harness and helmet. "Just right. Both of you."

They followed her over to a wooden platform. At the ladder, Audrey tipped her head back and looked up and up. She hadn't counted on a ladder.

"You go up first," Hudson said. "I'll be right behind you. If you slip, I'll be right there to catch you."

Audrey appreciated that he could say that without sounding patronizing. She blew out a breath. "Okay. Up we go."

The staff woman went first, clambering up with the agility of a monkey. Audrey ignored that, and put one foot on the ladder.

Hudson was right at her shoulder, close enough that if she leaned back, just an inch or two, she'd be touching him. "Just take your time. I'm right here." He gripped the ladder on either side of her. But instead of making her feel crowded, it made her feel safe.

She began to climb. It took an embarrassingly long time, but she didn't slip, didn't have any trouble with her footing. And if she enjoyed the periodic brush of Hudson's body against hers as he climbed up almost directly behind her, who could blame her for that?

The staff woman helped her up onto the platform and immediately snapped the safety line onto the rigging above their heads. Even so, Audrey scooted to the massive post in the center and wrapped her arms around it. "Holy crap, this is high."

Hudson leapt lightly onto the platform behind her. "You got a heights thing?"

"It's never come up before." Why would it? She'd never been outdoorsy and the highest she'd been was at mountain overlooks or skyscrapers, behind nice, solid safety railings and windows.

"You're gonna be just fine. Taylor here has you all tied in."

"Can you maybe go first?" There was only a little bit of squeak to her voice.

"Sure can."

Taylor attached him to the zipline.

"Now here's how this works. You're going to step off the edge here."

Audrey's stomach dipped as she glanced toward the ground far below, then quickly pulled her gaze back up.

"Look at me. Just at me," Hudson ordered.

Audrey did as he asked, focusing on those calm, dark gray eyes, and felt herself settle.

"You'll feel just a little dip as the line takes your weight. Then you're just gonna slide down. You might twist a bit in the wind, depending on your balance. But you won't fall, and you won't hit anything. They keep all this ruthlessly maintained. At the other end, there will be a ramp angling up to the top of the next platform. You'll slow down as you get there and hit the ramp running, then slow your own momentum from there. The center pole the line is attached to will be wrapped in padding if you don't slow down fast enough, and I'll be right there waiting. Okay?"

It was the same soothing tone he'd used on her at the accident site. Telling her everything would be okay. And it had been. This was nothing compared to that.

"Okay. See you on the other side."

He flashed a grin at her in an unexpectedly boyish burst of excitement. "I'll be waiting." Then he stepped off the platform, backward.

His whoop echoed through the trees as the zipper thing carried him away from her. Before he left her sight, she saw him swing his legs up, wrapping them around the center line so he was flying upside down.

"Yeah, don't do that," Taylor told her.

"Don't worry. I won't!"

"You ready?"

Hudson would be waiting.

"Yeah."

"One, two…"

On three, Audrey stepped off the platform. She let out a little shriek at the momentary sensation of falling before the line caught. Then she was flying through the air, the trees zipping by. And it was *thrilling!* The forest opened up around her and she realized she was zooming across a little valley. It stretched out below her, pretty as a postcard before more woods swallowed her again. In the distance, she saw the next platform, saw the ramp she was aiming for. And she saw Hudson waiting. Audrey was already pedaling her feet, searching for purchase as she came in, faster than she expected. Taking the sudden weight of her body had her pitching forward, into a stumbling run. But Hudson caught her, as promised, wrapping his arms around her and absorbing the last of the momentum.

Audrey's breath wooshed out.

"You did it!" He grinned down at her, his eyes sparkling.

"Yes, I did!" Adrenaline pumped through her system, and it was the most natural thing in the world to follow the excitement and throw her arms around his shoulders, pressing her lips to his.

His mouth was warm and firm and tasted faintly of mint. And it didn't soften under hers. In fact, he didn't move a muscle—not to pull her closer or push her away. The shock of what she'd done rippled through her and Audrey froze. A second later she dropped back to her feet, her face feeling like a five-alarm fire. "Um. Sorry about that."

She couldn't look at him as she stepped out of his arms. He didn't fight to keep her there.

"No worries." His tone was easy, unconcerned, as if women threw themselves at him every day. Maybe they did. "Want to go again?"

Yes, yes, I would, but I wish you'd kiss me back.

But he was talking about ziplining. And yeah, she wanted to do that again, too. Not meeting the eyes of the staff member manning this particular platform, she just nodded and let him switch her over to the next line. Then, without a word, she jumped and hoped the wind would cool the mortification still flaming in her cheeks.

AT THE END of the zipline course, Audrey made excuses to get back to camp. Hudson let her because he needed the space. Neither of them had made eye contact since that kiss. He knew she was embarrassed, and he felt like a dick leaving the giant elephant between them. But drawing attention to it would only make things worse. It couldn't happen again. She made him forget, made him feel good, and he didn't deserve that. When she rode the golf cart back to camp proper, he opted to walk.

He'd hoped it would clear his head. But all he managed was several instant replays, where he responded to that soft, sweet mouth on his. Needing to get himself grounded, he slipped out his phone, chancing that this high up, he might have enough signal to check-in on John.

One bar. Probably not enough for a call, but he could still text.

Hey Rach. Just checking in. How is he today?

The reply came back as Hudson was cresting the ridge, bringing the central camp buildings into view.

Rachel: **The same. Why are you texting? You're not supposed to have your phone.**

Hudson: **You can always reach me. You know that.**

Rachel: **You're on vacation. Act like it.**

Seriously? Did she, of all people, think he'd be able to switch everything off and just go on living as if his best friend, his brother of the heart, wasn't lying, unresponsive in a hospital bed?

His phone pinged with another text.

Rachel: **He'd be pissed you're doing this, you know.**

Then he could damned well wake up and tell Hud so himself.

Hudson: **I love you both.**

Rachel: **We know. Love you back. Go play.**

Play. He'd done that for a precious stretch this morning. Focused on this place, this woman—both far removed from home and work and tragedy. He felt guilty as hell about forgetting, even for a moment, but Audrey's infectious enthusiasm was a drug he wanted another hit of.

Well, now he had fresh guilt to add to the pile. He couldn't shake the sense that he owed Audrey an apology. Not that he knew exactly how to say it. *Look, I'm sorry I didn't kiss you back the way I wanted. It's not you, it's me. My life is a mess, I'm an asshole, and you don't actually want to be involved with me.*

Right. That would make her feel better.

She was better off if he stayed away. He managed to convince himself of that for at least a few hours, but by late afternoon, he sought her out. Even if he'd mucked up the nascent friendship— or whatever the hell was between them—he needed to know she was okay. After the highly physical morning, Hudson expected Audrey would be hanging in the crafts hut or the pottery studio. He remembered how excited she'd been about getting her hands dirty. Instead, he found her at the ropes course, strapping on yet another helmet and harness.

Well, you go girl. He stood for a long moment, admiring her moxie. Then, before he could think better of it, he was asking if there was room for one more.

"The hermit emerges," Charlie quipped.

"We aren't all as social as you," Hudson retorted.

Sam gave him a long, speculative look, but not the *eat shit and die* glare he expected. So maybe Audrey hadn't said anything about the kiss. Considering the speed with which she was attempting to climb that ladder and get away from him, it looked like she was still embarrassed.

Ready to leap into action, he kept a sharp eye on her until she made it up to the first perch. Then he slipped into his own safety gear and went up after her. His greater height and reach gave him an advantage in catching up. Whereas Charlie and Sam went straight for the upper levels of the course, Audrey was being smart and starting with the easier obstacles. So at least her desire to get away from him wasn't overriding good sense.

He left her to it, circling around from the other side as she worked her way through each section. Only when she made it to the upper reaches, to the tougher part, did he draw near. By then all her concentration was on foot placement and hand-holds. He made it to the top ahead of her and waited, watching as she slowly picked her way across the net bridge. Far below, Sam and Charlie shouted encouragement, having already finished their run.

Audrey was trembling with exhaustion. Hudson could see it as she made it to the next perch. One obstacle left to get to the end. The hardest.

"You can do it, Audrey!" Sam called.

"I'll need a nap after this," Audrey answered. She took a moment to catch her breath, then stretched out her arm, reaching for the next bar. It was several inches out of her grasp.

"You'll have to take the leap," he said, not so loud that those on the ground could hear.

She didn't take her focus off her goal. After a long moment, she said, "Tried that once today. Didn't end so well."

So, she had heard him.

"Took me by surprise."

Audrey looked at him then, a mix of exasperation and disbelief on her features. "Really? You're gonna go with that?"

"It's the truth." But it wasn't the whole truth. "Look, this morning wasn't about you. I'm...dealing with some stuff." He knew he couldn't just leave it there. "Make it over here to the other side, and I'll tell you."

"Promise?"

He held up his hand in a Boy Scout salute. "I'm a man of my word."

Audrey seemed to consider that for a long moment. Then she nodded, her eyes going back to the bars. She was too short to make it easily, but it was clear she was about to try. Hudson readied himself to retrieve her if she missed one of the narrow rungs that crossed the chasm and ended up dangling from her safety harness. Still, he wasn't prepared when she jumped for the first handhold. He sucked in a breath. But her fingers closed around it, leaving her dangling, feet nowhere near the row of steps across the bottom. Her legs swung, her arms straining as she lurched forward, reaching for the next bar. She grabbed it. Amazed, Hudson watched as she repeated the performance, working her way across the final obstacle as if it were a set of elementary school monkey bars.

There was nothing more for her to grab onto at the final perch. Nothing except him. He opened his arms, waiting to catch her, wondering if her trust was so damaged that she'd rather not finish than do this. But Audrey didn't hesitate, pitching herself forward the last few feet to crash into him. Cheers went up from below. Hudson stepped back, tugging her away from the edge, out of view of their audience.

He ought to let her go. He'd done the bare minimum and caught her. But his arms wouldn't release, and he couldn't look away from her big blue eyes. Her adrenaline was up again. He could see it in the thump of her pulse, feel it in the tremble against his body. But she wasn't smiling this time. Neither was he. Somehow his hand lifted of its own volition, threading into the hair at her nape. Yeah, soft as it looked.

"Good job," he murmured.

Tension drew taut between them, and he knew he was going to kiss her. He shouldn't. But he'd damn himself later.

"Are you seeing somebody?" she blurted.

"Right now, I'm looking at you." At her fearless determination and refusal to accept limitations. It was sexy as hell.

"That's...that's not what I meant."

Hudson stroked a thumb along her cheek. "I'm not with anybody, no."

"Then perhaps we could have this conversation somewhere with a little less altitude. The way you're looking at me makes me dizzy."

He smiled a little at that. "Yeah, we can do that. You up for a walk?"

"Lead the way."

CHAPTER 8

*A*UDREY KNEW THERE WAS a chance she'd just ruined her shot at another kiss, but she was pretty sure he was entirely capable of scrambling her brain and distracting her, and she needed to know his story. They made their way to the bottom of the course. Thank God there were stairs down from the top. She didn't think she had it in her to navigate the whole thing again to get back to the start. She'd probably overdone it again, but she'd *done* it—made it all the way from beginning to end, through every single obstacle—and she was proud of that. Hudson looked proud, too. Though, why should he? She was nothing to him.

He challenged that assumption when he took her hand, after they turned in their gear. Sam and Charlie, predictably, disappeared at that, saying they'd catch up at dinner later and making all kinds of suggestive eyebrow waggles behind Hudson's back. Audrey thought he'd let her go once he tugged her away from the ropes course, but he kept his fingers curved around hers, connected, at least superficially. In truth, she felt more than superficially connected to him, and that was dangerous territory. Except, he'd come back, seeking her out this afternoon, despite what had happened at the zipline. In the wake of all his rescues, that had to mean…something. Right?

"I'm sorry about this morning," he said.

"Which part?" The question slipped out before she could stop it. But since when had she ever avoided asking the difficult questions?

"Right now, it's an even split between not kissing you back and letting you walk off embarrassed."

Well. That was more honesty than she'd expected.

"You said it wasn't about me and that you aren't with anyone. Are you in the middle of a divorce?" It was one explanation that had occurred to her as she hung forty feet above the ground.

"No. Never married. Not coming out of any other relationship either."

Okay, so she hadn't been unintentionally poaching in someone else's territory. Which left what? The possibilities circled around her brain as he led her toward the gazebo by the lake, her analytical mind taking what she'd seen, what he'd said, and turning over the pieces, trying to make them fit. As they stepped into the shade of the gazebo, she voiced her conclusion. "You lost someone."

His head snapped toward her.

"You weren't calm and collected after the fire the other night. It wasn't the fire itself, because you didn't hesitate. It was that you thought I was hurt. Since you've been doing the job for years, the only way that made sense was that something happened on the job."

Hudson's eyes narrowed. "What exactly is it you're a professor of?"

"Sociology. I study broader trends in the development, structure, and functioning of human society, not individuals." Though she'd taken enough graduate courses in psychology out of her own interests to complete a master's degree. "But I am someone who's been on the outside for most of my life. I'm good at observing people. You're hurting. You're good at hiding it, but you're hurting."

He just stared at her, saying nothing, for long enough that her shoulders began to twitch.

"What?"

"I'm just wondering, if I wait long enough, if you'll guess the rest."

"That's as far as I've gotten." She squeezed the hand she still held. "Tell me what's going on, Hudson."

He released her hand and turned away, leaning his forearms on the railing and looking out over the water. "I shouldn't be here."

"With me? At camp?"

"Alive."

Whatever Audrey had expected, it wasn't that. She moved up beside him and mirrored his position, close, but not touching, and waited.

"Three months ago, my company got called to a structure fire. Multi-story apartment building. Three of us were on the roof. Me, John, and Steve. We've been tight since diapers. Done everything together. School. Firefighter academy. Joined the same company when we finished. We were a unit."

She didn't miss his use of the past tense.

"Shit was getting dicey, but there was a woman trapped in a corner room on the back side of the building. We were trying to get a handle on the blaze, redirect it so our people could get to her. But things took a turn." Hudson closed his eyes, his face twisting.

Audrey couldn't stop herself from laying a hand on his where it curved over the rail. It was hard as iron beneath her touch.

"The roof collapsed on us. Steve and I fell through. I hit the top floor landing. Steve crashed through the railing and fell all the way to the lobby below. Four stories."

She felt her heart twist and bleed with all the emotions he wasn't letting into his voice.

"I was out of it from the fall. Dislocated my shoulder, sprained some shit. Didn't know which way was up. Probably would've tried to go down the stairs, even though it was too late for Steve. John came down after me. He—well the details don't matter. He got me out. But before he could get out himself, more of the roof collapsed." Hudson's throat worked as he swallowed. "The rest of the company got him out, but he sustained some pretty awful head trauma. He's been in a coma ever since." He turned toward her, and the grief in his eyes all but brought Audrey to her knees. "I walked away because of him."

She wrapped her arms around him, holding tight. She didn't say a word, didn't offer false platitudes or "It'll be okays." Because who knew if it would? She just hung on, pressing her cheek against his heart. "I'm so sorry."

He folded her in, wrapping his arms tight around her and burying his face in her hair. She had the impression he hadn't had —or let himself have—any comfort. It was clear he still blamed himself. And instead of embracing his second chance at life, as she had, he'd shut himself off. That made her heart ache for him. He felt such wells of grief, and she couldn't fix it.

Eventually he pulled back enough to look down at her. "I don't know why I told you that."

He'd made her a deal, but Audrey knew if he really hadn't wanted to tell her, he'd have found a way around it. "Because I've also been through stuff. You were there for part of it, so you know. And sometimes, you just have to talk about it. To get it out."

"I'm a guy. We don't talk about feelings."

"I won't tell anybody." It was part teasing, part serious. She'd keep what he told her in confidence. "But it doesn't change the fact that you have to deal with what you feel. I don't want to make you feel guilty." No camp fling was worth that.

Hudson lifted a hand to her cheek, searching her face. "I feel a lot of things when I'm with you. Guilt isn't one of them."

She arched a brow. "So, you feel guilty about that?"

He gave a wry smile. "Yeah. Then I felt guilty for letting you walk away."

Her heart gave a hard bump under hear breastbone. "I'm not walking away now."

"I should." But he didn't move.

"Hudson."

"Yeah?"

"Maybe you should just acknowledge we both need this." Because this thing growing between them—whatever it was—had moved well past just wanting, well past the simple.

The corner of his mouth tipped up. "Are you always this rational?"

"Usually."

"Thank God." He closed the distance between them, settling his mouth firmly over hers.

Audrey sighed into the kiss, relaxing against him when he pulled her closer. His body was hard and hot, but his mouth…his mouth was a sweet seduction. No rush, no impatient escalation, just a bone-melting assault on her senses. She'd never been kissed like this, never even imagined this existed outside the pages of a book or a Hollywood screen. Like she was the center of his world and he had an eternity just to explore her mouth.

When he eased back, she sagged, hanging onto him for balance.

Instantly concerned, he shifted his grip to better support her. "You okay? Are your knees hurting?"

"Nope. I just don't have any anymore. You dissolved them."

The rumble of his chuckle felt delicious. "You're good for my ego."

Audrey had a feeling he'd be good for her everything. And that was just a little bit terrifying. She turned her focus back to stiffening her legs so she wasn't hanging onto Hudson like a limp noodle. Now that she thought about it, the exhaustion from her day's exertion was starting to make itself felt. She hadn't been kidding about needing a rest earlier.

As if reading her mind, he wrapped an arm around her waist. "How about we find one of those two-person hammocks and take a little nap?"

Snuggling up against that big, warm body and snoozing? "That sounds...perfect."

HUDSON DIDN'T KNOW QUITE how it had happened, but he was smack dab in the middle of a camp fling. Well, okay, he knew how. He'd kissed Audrey and quickly discovered one taste would never be enough. But he didn't know how he'd gotten to a place where he wasn't beating himself up about that.

There'd still been no change with John's condition. After assuring Hudson that she'd contact him the moment there was anything worth reporting, Rachel had threatened total radio silence if he didn't actually focus on his vacation. So, he'd focused on Audrey. It had been a blast. Somehow, when he was with her, his world felt—not okay, exactly, but less out of balance. And since they'd spent every waking minute together for the last three days, he was feeling—dare he admit it?—happy, for the first time since the fire.

"That's what you're wearing to go canoeing?" He eyed her cargo pants and long-sleeved t-shirt. "You do know it's June, right?"

"I also know I'm a red-head, and I'll be applying SPF 100 all day." She added a wide-brimmed hat to the outfit. It should've looked ridiculous. Mostly, he just thought she was adorable.

He had yet to see her in anything but long pants. Fair complexion aside, he figured her legs were pretty scarred from the accident and subsequent surgeries. It wouldn't be surprising if she were sensitive about that. "And if we go in the water?"

"I've got a swimsuit on underneath. Although you assured me you're good at this, so I'm not anticipating getting wet."

His brain went off on a highly inappropriate mental detour at that. They were paddling out to the island in the middle of the lake. Total privacy. He wasn't taking her out there with the express purpose of getting her naked, but...the island did have a reputation. He was willing to bet that big brain of hers had precluded her from having quite a few of the more typical high school experiences. If she wanted to cross a few off the list, who was he to deny a lady?

"Hudson?"

"Yeah?"

Her mouth quirked, as if she knew exactly where his mind had gone. "I said do we have everything?"

"Pretty sure." He'd already stowed the picnic the camp kitchen had packed for them, along with a blanket and first aid kit. "You ready?"

"Always."

He loved that Audrey was game for anything, ready and willing to grab life by the horns. Such a different response to nearly dying. Then again, nobody else had died or nearly died because of her. Hudson shoved that thought away and helped her into a life jacket, lingering a little over the checking of the straps so he could tug her in for a fast kiss.

She was grinning as he set her back on her feet. "I like that part of the safety check."

"You'll want to keep a low center of gravity to avoid tipping." He handed her into the canoe.

She bobbled a little, then crouched and planted her butt in the seat.

Hudson climbed into the stern, taking up his paddle and pushing them away from the dock. "You hold your paddle like this—one hand curled over this little cross piece at the top, the other down here, close to the juncture of the blade and the shaft."

Not a good enough reason for using the word shaft, he thought, as his brain offered up a flood of images that had Audrey wrapping her hands around *his* shaft.

Hudson's voice was a little rougher when he spoke again. "You're going to turn your torso so the paddle side shoulder is forward and dip the blade into the water, perpendicular to the canoe. Then drag it back through the water in a long, smooth stroke." His cock jumped as he demonstrated the proper technique. *Jesus, when did everything about canoeing turn sexual?*

"Like this?" she asked, mimicking his movement.

"Don't come back quite so far. You want to stop each stroke about your hip. And you'll swap sides every few strokes. Try to use your core strength, not your back, or you'll regret it later."

After a little more practice, she had the technique down—and thank God. All this talk of shafts and strokes and proper rhythm had his board shorts uncomfortably tight.

They lapsed into companionable silence as they worked out their paddling cadence and made their way down the lake.

"Where are we headed?"

"Blueberry Island. Best place around for a picnic. Quiet, secluded, no cabinmates hanging around to be nosy and annoying. And if we're lucky, the wild blueberries haven't been wiped out by wildlife yet."

"Mmm. And how many girls did you take there to get lucky back when you were at camp?"

"I was fourteen when camp closed for good."

"So, you're saying you never took a girl out here?"

"Well, I might have brought Claudia Collingsworth out one night in the hope of scaring her pantsless with ghost stories."

Audrey snorted. "I gather you were unsuccessful?"

"Only partly. I got to second base, before a noise convinced her that Big Foot was coming to kill us both, and she ran screaming back to the boat."

She threw back her head and laughed, the sound rolling over him like a wave. He couldn't even be annoyed that it was at his expense.

"I never did anything so normal."

"I guess the age-gap between you and your classmates made dating pretty hard."

"I was, shall we say, a late bloomer. Dating mostly just didn't happen. Age-gap aside, nobody wanted to date the freak." She said it with the kind of ease that told him she regularly used the term, and Hudson found it really pissed him off.

"You're not a freak."

"You're sweet to get insulted on my behalf." He could hear the smile in her voice. "But I was. I barely existed on the same planet as my peers. The people in my age group were intimidated as hell. The people who were intellectual peers either didn't look at me twice because they considered me a child or resented the hell out of the fact that I'd gotten where they were so much sooner than they had. I had no idea how to be normal. That's more than half the reason I went into sociology. I was trying to understand how society was supposed to work, to figure out how I fit. And the truth was, I didn't. So, I didn't date. Not really."

It was such a bleak picture and didn't at all fit how he saw her. How had she turned out so warm and open and well-adjusted? She'd just described an almost total lack of relationships with people her own age for a huge chunk of her life. He couldn't imagine that. Couldn't imagine the years without John and Steve. He couldn't imagine it now, and it was needing to face that reality that had brought him to his knees after the fire and kept him there.

He swallowed past the lump in his throat. "Sounds lonely."

"It was." She said it without an ounce of self-pity. Just a simple statement of fact. "It's only been in the past few years, as everybody else started catching up with me in their own education and career paths, that it stopped mattering so much. I'm old enough now that it's not weird I have a PhD, and most people don't think to ask. Not that dating has been on my radar at all since the accident. The guy I was seeing when it happened rapidly disappeared, and I spent pretty much every waking minute in physical therapy."

"Wait a minute. The guy you were dating bailed on you after the accident?"

"After the first surgery. He wasn't prepared to deal with someone who'd be permanently disabled."

Hudson's hands fisted on the paddle. "I'd like to permanently disable him. What a dick."

"He was. He didn't love me, and I didn't love him. So, it all worked out all right in the end. I think that's part of why I fought so hard to walk again. Not because I was worried no one would ever want to be with me if I couldn't, but just as a kind of 'fuck you' to Lance. That and I didn't want to be dependent on my parents for the rest of my life. Don't get me wrong," she rushed on, as if she'd just insulted the Pope. "My parents are amazing, and I love them. But they liked being needed again way too much. They both had an epic case of empty nest syndrome when I finished school."

"I think a lot of parents have a hard time remembering how to have an identity outside of being a parent once their kids are grown. That's probably worse with yours, since you'd have been so young when you went through college and grad school. I'm guessing they stayed way more involved than parents usually do at those stages."

"Did yours? Have the empty nest thing, I mean."

"Not with me. My baby sister was still around for another four years, and she was something of a hell raiser, so I think my dad was grateful to see her out on her own and thankful for whatever hair he had left at that point. Mom's a teacher, so I think she gets her fill of parenting still with her students. But it doesn't stop them from wanting to be involved or doing what they think I need. They're why I'm here. Mom thought camp would be good for me. Probably because it's one of the few things I did growing up without John and Steve."

Audrey was quiet for a minute, smoothly dragging her paddle through the water. "Has it been good for you?"

"You have." No reason to pussy foot around that.

"I'm glad." Her voice was soft.

Hudson wished he could see her face. They hadn't talked about what they were doing here. They'd just been living in the moment, enjoying each other. Simple. Uncomplicated.

Except if this had been just a simple fling, he'd never have told her about the fire. And nothing about the pull he felt toward her was uncomplicated. It was all bound up in their shared history and a strangely compelling desire to protect her. To keep doing what he could to put that look of excitement and pleasure on her face.

Audrey cleared her throat. "Can I ask you something?"

"Sure."

"Could you—oh my God! Snake! Snake!" She shot to her feet, rocking the canoe.

Hudson immediately dropped lower, trying to counter her shifting weight. "You're going to tip us. Sit down."

"There's a *snake* at my feet," she squeaked.

"Okay, calm down. Sit back—"

She tried to step backward on the bow seat, rocking the boat until water sloshed over the edge.

"Don't!" But his warning came too late. The canoe lurched and Audrey tumbled straight into the lake.

CHAPTER 9

"*I*T WAS JUST A little rat snake that had crawled under the seat to take a nap. They don't bite."

Audrey sent Hudson a withering glare. "It was a slithering thing *at my feet.*"

He wisely refrained from further comment, instead pulling a hamper and blanket from the canoe. Because, of course, *he* hadn't gone overboard. No, just her.

Soaking wet and irritated with her own over-reaction, she unsnapped the life jacket and yanked it off, dumping it into the beached canoe. Now they were about to hike to...somewhere, and she was going to chafe all over the place.

"C'mon."

With as much dignity as she could muster—which was to say, none—she headed in the direction he indicated. God, she was embarrassed. But it was *a snake.* Hadn't he ever seen *Indiana Jones?* Didn't he understand the horror?

"So, you were going to ask me something?" he prompted.

Oh, hell no. No way could she ask him *now.* She looked like a total spaz. She was not about to still ask him if he'd be interested in checking off some of those bases with her, attraction be damned. But God, she'd been thinking about his hands all during their little paddling lesson, and then she'd stayed hot and bothered—at least until her unplanned dunk in the lake. She'd even been a little bit jealous of Claudia Collingsworth for having had those hands on her. Okay, maybe a lot jealous. Audrey knew how stirred up Hudson's kisses got her. She couldn't stop wondering about the rest. When Sam had tossed out the idea of a flaming hot affair, Audrey hadn't given it any serious thought. But now…

"Never mind. It was nothing."

"You're thinking awfully hard about nothing. And it's making you blush."

Damn her red-head's complexion! Couldn't a woman be embarrassed without announcing it to the world?

The little island was heavily forested, so she said nothing and concentrated on walking, so she didn't add tripping over a root or a hole or her own damned feet to her list of mortifications for the day. After all the exertion the last few days, that required a lot more effort than she liked. The hike to the center of the island didn't take more than five or ten minutes. It was a tiny island, after all. The little clearing reminded her of a fairy bower—which made her feel excessively romantic and stupid. Fairy bower? She was a scientist. A logical, rational professional. But the impression remained, with trees wrapping around the space in a way that suggested utter privacy.

Hudson flipped out the blanket and spread it out over the grass. "Pretty, isn't it?"

"If I were a Disney princess, I'd open my mouth to sing and small woodland creatures would scurry to the edge to pay homage."

He laughed. "You don't strike me as the Disney princess type."

"They were my guilty pleasure growing up. Intellectually, I get all the problems with some of the messages they put out there for girls, but I certainly never watched *Beauty and the Beast* and thought 'oh hey, Stockholm Syndrome seems like a good idea' or that I should change what made me me for the sake of some guy after watching *The Little Mermaid*. I just loved the stories and the music."

"Which one is your favorite?"

"Honestly? *Sleeping Beauty*. Which ought to be ridiculous. Aurora has literally eighteen lines of dialog in the entire movie. And *Tangled*. I guess I relate to the whole princess removed from the normal world. And the overprotective parent vibe." Why had she said that? It made her sound pitiful.

"I was much more into *Shrek*. An animated movie with fart jokes? It was great. Plus, Eddie Murphy. I love all things Eddie Murphy. I used to be able to quote *The Nutty Professor* word for word."

Audrey snorted. She toed off her shoes and started to step onto the blanket.

"You might as well strip down and lay out your clothes to dry. They have to be uncomfortable."

They were, but she didn't move.

"If you hang them up now, they'll probably be dry by the time we head back. Plus, it's shady enough here, you shouldn't burn," he continued, peeking into the hamper.

She still didn't budge.

"Unless you were lying about having a swimsuit on under there?"

She did have a swimsuit. A bikini. One that had once made her feel sexy. But that was before. She'd only packed it for camp because buying another seemed a waste of money, and she hadn't really planned on doing any water stuff anyway because she had no intention of showing her legs. Ever. They invited too many questions, too much pity.

And yet she was thinking about being intimate with this man. That would require exposing her scars—both literal and metaphorical. Could she do that? Could she really trust him enough, let him in that far? Hudson knew what she'd been through. Part of it, anyway. They wouldn't be a surprise to him. And maybe this was a good, safe way to test herself. To see how she felt about someone seeing her.

I can do this.

Before she could lose her nerve, Audrey tossed her hat onto the blanket and stripped off her shirt. She hung it on a branch, then unbuttoned her pants and slipped them off, too. But she couldn't make herself turn around to see his face. Her heart pounded in a sickening rhythm, too loud in her ears, and her skin prickled with more than just gooseflesh. She wanted to grab up the blanket and wrap it around herself, anything to cover back up. But she stood in the silence, biting her lip, until she couldn't stay quiet anymore.

"They basically had to rebuild my legs. Multiple surgeries and about twenty pounds' worth of pins, rods, plates, new knees... It's functional but not very pretty. Sort of Bride of Frankenstein. With better hair."

Audrey jumped when Hudson's hands skimmed down her arms. She hadn't heard him move.

"You know what I see when I look at you?" he asked softly.

"No." She could barely force the word out.

He turned her to face him, tipping her chin to force her to look up at him. Stubborn, she kept her eyes downcast, somewhere around his mouth.

"Strength. And that's the sexiest thing I can imagine."

Her heart flipped. She wanted to believe that, but she just... couldn't. "That's sweet, but—"

"I'm not lying to make you feel better, Audrey." He reeled her in, pulling her flush against his body until the truth of his statement nudged her in the belly.

"Oh!" Heat swept through her at the contact.

Audrey lifted her eyes to his and lost her breath. He wanted her. The huge erection was certainly a clue, but he could've been thinking about some hot model or a bikini car wash or any

number of things that might turn him on. But he was looking at
her, as if he wanted to devour her. It made her knees go weak.
How was it he could see anything other than a woman broken?

Hudson cupped her cheek, sliding his hand into her hair. "Let
me show you."

Had she spoken aloud? Before she had a chance to think about
it, he'd lowered his lips to hers. They'd shared several kisses over
the past few days, some initiated by him, some by her. They'd
varied from hot to playful to sweet. But this. This was something
else entirely.

He made love to her mouth. It was all she could think as he
slowly stripped away her anxiety and embarrassment, leaving
nothing behind but needs. She realized, as he lowered her to the
blanket, that her sexual experiences before had been pale substi-
tutes for what could be. She'd thought this kind of pleasure was a
fiction, a fairy tale. The sort of thing that existed only in dreams.
If this was a dream, she didn't ever want to wake up.

His hands roamed over her, impossibly gentle as he skimmed
those calloused fingers across her skin. How could such big,
powerful hands be so reverent? They made her feel cherished,
electric. And when his palms cupped her breasts, she arched into
the touch, desperate for more. He tore his mouth from hers, and
she whimpered at the loss, until he pressed his lips to the column
of her throat, thumbs stroking her nipples through the swimsuit.
Everything in her went taut.

Audrey tipped her head back to give him better access,
threading her fingers into the hair at his nape as he kissed his way
down to the little hollow above her collarbone and continued to
massage her breasts. They were full and heavy in his hands, the
nipples pearled tight and sensitive. With every brush of his
thumbs, her sex pulled tighter.

"More," she breathed and couldn't even care that it came out a
plea.

His fingers tugged at the knot of straps behind her neck until the bow released, then drew them down with slow deliberation. The sun on her bare breasts was nothing compared to the heat of his gaze as he looked at her.

"Beautiful."

He drew her into his mouth, circling her nipple with his tongue, and Audrey all but flew off the blanket. Hudson shifted, nudging one muscular thigh between hers, pressing right against her aching center, and, oh, that was better. Her hips began to move to the same, suckling rhythm he set with his mouth. Breath catching, she speared her hands in his hair, holding him to her when he shifted to the other breast. God, she was so close he was going to make her come, just from this.

"Hudson." His name came out on a moan.

He worked one hand between them, cupping her. Audrey arched into the touch with a cry. So. Very. Close. She widened her legs and bucked into his hand. He came back to her mouth, thrusting his tongue against hers as he rubbed the heel of his palm against her mound, and she shattered.

He held her through the shuddering aftermath, bringing her down with long, drugging kisses, and easy strokes of his hands.

"Okay?" he asked.

No. She was pretty sure he'd just ruined her for all men, and they hadn't even had sex yet. "That was...I don't...You're really good at that."

Hudson chuckled and the rumble of it shot straight to her still quivering core. "Not done yet."

"You're not?" she asked weakly.

In answer, he blew on her nipples, still wet from his mouth, and she felt herself stir again. This just might kill her, but oh, what a way to go.

He kissed his way down her torso, lingering at the edge of her bikini bottoms. She wondered if he'd pull them off with his teeth. That mental image caused a fresh flood of warmth. But he didn't take them off. Not yet, anyway. He ran a finger just inside the top edge. That only made her think of it going lower, deeper.

Oh yes, please.

But he didn't do that either. Instead, he kissed his way down her hip to her thigh, taking his time, continually skimming those gentle hands along her skin. As he neared her knee, she tensed.

He paused to look up at her again. "Still okay?"

She wanted this, wanted what he was trying to give her. She couldn't let her neuroses get in the way of that. "Yeah." But she dropped her head back to the blanket, not ready to watch him as he worked his way down the rest of her legs, over all the scar tissue. She'd just focus on the sensation of his mouth, his hands. Nothing else. She closed her eyes.

He straightened her leg, lifting it up, and she waited for the feather-soft kisses. When none came, she murmured, "Don't stop."

Still nothing.

Was he waiting for some acknowledgment?

Audrey lifted her head to look down at him. He *was* kissing her, somewhere around her ankle. In dawning horror, she stared, watching him work his way back toward her knee.

Her throat went tight. "I can't." There were tears at the edge of her voice, but she couldn't stop them.

Hudson's attention snapped toward her, a frown bowing those masterful lips. "Audrey?"

"I can't," she repeated, feeling hysteria bubbling up in her chest.

He laid her leg down on the blanket, covering it with his palm in a gesture that was probably meant to be comforting. "It's okay. It's fine. We don't have to do anything you don't want to do."

"No!" She sucked in a breath and let the rest out on a sob. "I can't feel that. I can't feel you touching me."

WHAT THE HELL had just happened?

Minutes ago, she'd been moaning with pleasure, gone limp with the aftermath of a good, hard orgasm. Hudson had been good with that. Great with it. She'd looked so uncertain, so self-conscious about her scars, he'd just wanted to do something to make her realize how desirable she really was. Hell yes, he wanted her. He was still breathing and she was…amazing. Not because of that devastating intelligence—though that was sexy, too—but because of what she'd endured, how she'd come out stronger and so full of thirst for life. Those scars on her legs represented excruciating pain, both from the accident and the surgeries and physical therapy after. She still hurt, though she didn't let it slow her down. He had no idea how much being around him made her think of the accident, but he'd wanted to replace those thoughts, those memories, with pleasure—however much of it she'd allow. And now he'd gone and fucked it up. Instead of the pleasure, she'd remember this.

"Are you hurting?"

She shook her head, big, fat tears rolling down her cheeks. That just killed him. Hudson was pretty sure he'd rather be waterboarded than know he'd had anything to do with making her cry. He should've gone with his first instinct days ago and stayed away from her. This was just further proof that he wasn't fit to take care of anyone right now. But it was too late to turn back. He'd let her pull him out of his funk, let himself feel like a normal guy, who could have an uncomplicated fling. Now, they were in this together, and he'd messed up. He had to do something.

Praying he wasn't about to make this a thousand times worse, he stroked a hand down her leg, knee to ankle. "What do you feel?" He kept his voice calm, though his guts were tied in knots.

"I…nothing. It's just numb."

"Is it always numb?"

Audrey sat up, drawing her knees to her chest. She held the bikini top over her breasts, though she hadn't retied it. "I don't know. I still feel pain. How can I feel pain and nothing else?"

"Probably different nerves are responsible for those things." With all the surgeries, it made sense that there was considerable nerve damage. He stroked it again with firmer pressure, massaging muscles gone tense. "Can you feel the pressure?"

"A little."

"So, it's not so much the muscles as the skin. You're not feeling the surface stuff."

"I guess." She wiped at her eyes.

Taking that as a positive sign, he moved lower, running his hands over her bare foot. It flexed in his hands. "You felt that."

"Yes. I couldn't walk properly if I didn't. Well, I couldn't walk at all. I'm not sure what I do qualifies as proper."

"You walk. That's a miracle unto itself." Shifting to her other leg, he repeated the process, touching, testing. The feeling came back somewhere around her knees in both legs. Very gently, he pressed a kiss at the threshold where she could still feel sensation. "Do you want me to stop?"

Audrey stared at him.

Hudson brushed his lips over the inside of the other knee. "We can get dressed, go on back to camp and pretend this didn't happen." Not that he was going to forget the sounds she made when she came at any point in this lifetime. "We can have lunch, as we planned. Or...I can keep going. I can remind you of what you very definitely still feel."

She was frowning, looking down at his hands, and he realized he'd been idly rubbing them up and down her scarred calves.

He stilled, but didn't stop touching her. "Sorry."

"They...really don't bother you, do they? The scars." She sounded completely flummoxed by the idea.

"No. They're a part of you—arguably an indicator of the strongest part—but they're not all of you. I want *you*, Audrey. The whole package." He didn't have a right to want her. She was the sort of woman who deserved promises and forever. Someone who had his shit together and could stand by her. He wasn't that guy.

But right now, he could give her this. It had to be better than tears.

"Then don't stop." Throat working, she let the top fall, brushing a hesitant hand along his cheek. It cost her. Hudson could see that in the faint tremble that shook her hand. But she was taking the leap, as she'd done with everything else he'd thrown at her this week. He sure as hell planned to make sure she enjoyed the ride.

So, he kissed her. He kissed her like there was no tomorrow. Like there was no end to camp in a week. He kissed her until he lost himself in the taste of her mouth, the scent of her sun-warmed skin. She went pliant beneath him, relaxing, accepting— and it felt like a victory. Moving down her body, he used his hands, his mouth to coax her up again, steeping her in sensation. When he hooked his fingers in the waistband of her swimsuit, she moaned, "God, yes."

He peeled it off, baring her. She was lovely with all that flushed, alabaster skin. Hudson wanted to feast on it, on her, until they both found oblivion in pleasure. Skimming his palms up the outsides of her thighs, he watched her face as he bent low to press a kiss to her belly. It quivered as he edged lower, tracing her hipbone with his tongue. He expected her to close her eyes. Instead, she watched him, parting her legs to accommodate his shoulders. He settled between them, sliding his hands beneath her ass to drag her into better position. And he held her gaze as he lowered his mouth.

Audrey's breath exploded out, her body bowing in response to the slow lick of his tongue. She grabbed fistfuls of the blanket, gasping out his name. Her eyes stayed fixed on his, the pupils so huge, they swallowed up the blue. It was a shocking intimacy. More than the taste of her on his tongue, more than the feel of her heels digging into his shoulders. As if she saw that this wasn't entirely about her, but about losing himself in her pleasure, too.

Hudson couldn't look away. He soaked up every gasp, every

sigh, every needy whimper. And when he pushed her over the edge again, heard her scream, he felt a surge of triumph.

Audrey went boneless, eyes closing at last. With one last kiss to the inside of her thighs, he shifted to stretch out beside her. Sleepy, sated, she curled against him, one hand reaching for the waistband of his shorts.

Hudson caught it, brought to his mouth for little, nibbling kisses. "No."

Her eyes blinked open, not dazed at all despite the lethargic tone. "But what about you?"

"This wasn't about me. Today is all about you." His raging hard-on would fade. Eventually. He wasn't about to take advantage of her vulnerability. She needed some time to settle and process.

"That hardly seems fair."

He stroked a lazy hand from her waist to her hip, enjoying that she didn't seem self-conscious now. "I promise, I enjoyed that almost as much as you did."

"What did you get out of it?"

His lips curved, and he pressed another kiss to her bare shoulder. "The satisfaction of a job very well done."

"Cocky. But accurate." She closed her eyes and rode out another shudder. "So very accurate." Patting his chest, she rolled away, tugging her swimsuit back on.

There were still shadows in her eyes. He wanted to say something, to ask—shit, he didn't know what. How she was feeling? If she was really okay? But he didn't want to bring up the whole thing again and make it worse. So, he said nothing, watching her. As they fell on the picnic like they hadn't eaten in a week, Audrey said and did all the right things, laughing and joking with him. But as they packed up to head back to camp, he couldn't shake the feeling that her light was just a little bit dimmer.

CHAPTER 10

*A*UDREY COULDN'T SLEEP. RESTLESS, she retreated to the pottery studio. Probably there was some rule about being in here at night, without staff supervision. But she'd come often enough that she knew the ropes, how all the equipment worked. She wouldn't break anything. She just wanted some quiet time alone with the clay, to feel it beneath her hands. Switching on just a couple of the lamps on low, she perched on the stool and turned on the wheel. The steady whir of it soothed her. This was better than all the therapy she'd had after the accident. There was a distinct possibility she'd need a crate to pack up all the pieces she'd made since she got here.

She ached, in body and mind, both from overdoing it the last several days and from the discovery of yet another loss. There'd been so many in the wake of the accident. She didn't know why this one felt so huge, especially when she hadn't even known it was an issue until today. But it made her feel somehow incomplete. Yet another sign of being broken.

Hudson didn't think she was broken. And he'd certainly gone above and beyond to show her that she could absolutely still feel everywhere it counted. And dear God, how she'd felt. Just the thought of his mouth on her had her going wet and achy again. He'd given her the best orgasms of her life. She had the beard burn on her thighs to prove it. What did some lasting nerve damage mean in the face of that?

But he hadn't taken anything for himself. She didn't know how to feel about that. In truth, she didn't know how she felt about any of this, and for once her scientist's mind wasn't keen on analyzing it. She didn't want to be in this alone, didn't want to be the only one overwhelmed with feelings that were far too complex for a mere camp fling. She was in over her head, and she was deathly afraid that even Hudson couldn't save her from this.

The outside door opened. Audrey braced to explain her presence to camp security, but lost her train of thought when Hudson stepped into the room, as if summoned by her thoughts.

"I thought I might find you here."

Had she become so predictable? Maybe. She'd been in here every day since camp started.

He crossed over to lean against a bench, looking mouth-watering and sexy in low-slung jeans and a T-shirt. Beneath her hands, the vessel she was drawing up began to dip. In an effort to save it, she switched her attention back to her project and said nothing.

"You okay?"

She jerked her shoulder in a shrug, keeping her focus on the quiet whir of the wheel and the clay.

"I'm sorry."

Her gaze flickered to his, and she managed a small smile. "For what? The two mind-blowing orgasms? I think we both know I enjoyed them." Just looking at him had her legs going loose and heat gathering low in her belly. She'd happily spend the next week in his bed.

Hudson shifted. She wasn't used to seeing him as anything but fully self-assured and confident. "No. I just...I don't know if I handled things the best way today, and I just wanted to see if you were okay."

He was so sweet, and he wasn't the kind of guy you expected sweetness from. She didn't know why he cared, but it was obvious he did. And that did something to her, warming a long cold place in her chest. She could get used to that. Which was foolish, as there was no room for a future with him. Regardless of what choice she made, neither job option was anywhere close to Syracuse. She wasn't even sure how she'd feel going anywhere near the site of the accident. Not that it mattered. They hadn't broached the subject of whether this could be more than whatever it was. Come next week, they'd both go back to the real world, and they'd both have to find a way to be okay with that.

Because he seemed to need the reassurance, Audrey worked up a smile. "There's no need for apologies. I'm fine."

"You're upset or you wouldn't be in here in the middle of the night."

She could've pointed out what his own nocturnal wanderings said about his mental state, but deflection wasn't going to work on him. "I'm not upset." Being upset with reality was pointless.

"I know you better than that." The irritating truth was that he did. He understood her in a way few people ever had

But she didn t want to get into that. "Ever done pottery?"

"No."

"It's very therapeutic. Come sit with me. Get your hands dirty."

She didn't think he'd really do it. But after only a moment's hesitation, he crossed the room. She opened her mouth to tell him where all the supplies were located, but before she could speak, he'd dragged the stool from the next potter's wheel and sat behind her. It wasn't at all what she'd meant, but what red-blooded woman could sit in a pottery studio for a week and not have at least one fantasy about a Patrick Swayze in *Ghost* moment? So, Audrey went with it. "Give me your hands."

The hardness of his chest pressed into her back as he leaned forward, stretching his arms toward the wheel. She laid her hands over his and knew she'd be adding this to the roster of fantasies she'd begun to collect about them. She pressed his palms against the clay, deliberately collapsing the shape she'd begun in on itself. Starting over.

"I messed it up."

She thought maybe he was talking about more than the vase. "No. It was just a first attempt. Sometimes it takes a few tries to get it right." Reaching over, she dribbled more water on the clay. "What does it feel like?"

"Cool. Slick. There are lumps, but I can feel them smoothing out under my fingers."

Audrey felt her own rough edges smoothing out as his warm breath brushed her nape. "I love that feeling. It's very Zen. Like no matter how much of a mess things might be, if you stick with it, apply consistent pressure and effort—" She cupped his fingers and used them to mold the clay. "—eventually things get better." Reaching to the center of the lump, she pressed a thumb in, guiding his hands to draw it into a bowl shape.

"Not everything does."

"No," she agreed. "Sometimes things are just broken." She brought their hands in again, collapsing the shape.

"You aren't." The fierceness made her smile.

Because she didn't want to do anything else, she let herself relax back against him, let herself have the illusion that she'd always have this strong body to lean on. That idea was as seductive as his very talented mouth. "Not in any important way, no. It's not how I think of myself most of the time. But sometimes something happens that reminds me."

"Being around me this week has to be one gigantic reminder. I didn't think about that before today." His tone dripped with a regret that shocked her.

"No. You don't remind me of the accident. Not how you're thinking. You remind me that I'm still alive. That I'm still perfectly capable of living a full life. I don't feel broken when I'm with you. Because when you look at me, you actually see *me*. Not the aftermath of the accident. Not the girl genius. Me." He had from the beginning. Turning her head, she met his eyes and swallowed against a throat gone suddenly tight. "I'm going to miss the hell out of you when camp is over."

"Likewise." He flexed his fingers to curl with hers. Neither of them looked at the clay.

"Hudson."

"Yeah?"

The words piled up like a logjam in her throat, but she forced them out anyway. "Tell me this isn't just me."

He shook his head. "It's not just you."

Something loosened around her heart at that, even as a part of her thought of the ticking time clock. They had only days left together. How could that possibly be enough? "I don't know how to do this," she whispered. "I don't know how to keep this simple."

"Because we're not." He dropped his brow to hers. When he spoke again, his voice was deceptively light. "You know how you survive a camp romance?"

"How?" She needed all the survival tips she could get, because she knew that walking away from him, from this, would be brutal.

"You take the time you have and don't talk about the end of camp."

Accept that this was time out of time and embrace it. If that was the choice, she'd already made hers. Maybe she'd made her choice that first night on the pier. "Okay."

Hudson angled his head slightly. "Okay?"

"Then I'm all in. I want you—all of you—for whatever time we have left."

≈

OF COURSE, Audrey would choose to seize the day. Hudson should've realized that when he'd offered up the accepted wisdom for surviving camp romances. But there'd been a part of him hoping that she'd do what he couldn't and stop this thing between them before hearts got involved. Instead she'd offered him everything he wanted—for the next week, at least.

If this were a normal camp fling, following through would be a no-brainer. She was a beautiful woman, and he still had a pulse—currently drumming in his chest with anticipation. But this wasn't just a camp fling. They'd both already admitted to feeling more than they should, and taking this step would certainly reinforce that. There would be no going back, and he was positive that the week wouldn't be enough. But it wasn't in him to deny her anything. Not now. She was the only one who could still pull back. Hudson searched for the right words to get her to think about this one last time, without making her feel like it was a rejection. "Is that a good idea?"

She understood. Of course, she understood. "I've already told you I don't expect a permanent happy ending."

Maybe. But she deserved one. And that wasn't something he could give her—no matter how much he was starting to want to.

At his continued hesitation, she shifted, lifting her hand to his chest. "I'm not living my life for the future anymore, Hudson. I'm living it for the now. Because the now is the only thing you're ever guaranteed to have. You gave that back to me." She leaned into him, lifting her mouth a whisper from his. "Let me give this to you."

Right or wrong, he wasn't strong enough to walk away from this, from her. He started to lower his mouth to hers, then paused, holding his hands up. "Maybe after we wash off the mud."

Audrey blinked, then looked down where her palm had left a perfect print on the center of his t-shirt. Lips quirking, she slid off the stool, switching off the pottery wheel and heading for the sink. "Practicalities first."

She detoured to lock the door to the studio.

Hudson lifted a brow. "Here?"

"Unless *your* roommate is sleeping in someone else's cabin tonight?"

"Fair point." He ran through a quick mental list of camp locations for clandestine sex. Firefly Falls was too much of a hike and everywhere else he could think of carried too much risk of being caught. If they were doing this, the last thing he wanted was to be interrupted. Pottery studio it was.

He came up behind her at the sink, thrusting his hands beneath the running water, effectively trapping her. She squirted soap on her hands. Hudson pressed closer, nestling his erection against her luscious ass as he took those hands in his and slowly massaged the clay off.

Audrey hummed low in her throat and dropped her head forward. "This makes me wonder what magic you can work in a shower."

"We'll add it to the list." Taking advantage, he pressed a kiss to her exposed nape. "Personally, I really want the luxury of making love to you in a bed." And not just any bed, he realized. His bed. At home. It shocked him how easily he could picture her there, her hair spread out on his pillow, her body splayed out and limp from pleasure. But he didn't just see her in his bed. He saw her in his *life.* Cooking with him in his kitchen, laughing with his mom and sister, teasing the other guys at the fire house.

Audrey unzipped his jeans and slid her hand inside, wrapping those hot little fingers around his length, effectively wiping out his domestic fantasy. Hudson cursed, his hips bucking into her hand. Her lips curved into a wicked smile. "Oh, we'll find time for a bed. Because you've had your hands and mouth on every inch of me, and I really want to return the favor."

Whatever blood was left in his head drained south, as he imagined that pretty mouth wrapped around him, those big blue eyes staring up at him as she sucked him deep. Yeah, he'd perform whatever blackmail or magic was required to get them a bed. Preferably one where they wouldn't be interrupted for a solid twenty-four hours. That *might* be enough to slake this vicious thirst for her. For a little while.

"Hudson?"

"Yeah?" he croaked.

"You're wearing way too many clothes."

"So are you."

They dove at each other, tugging and tossing between desperate, fevered kisses, until they both stood naked. He watched, gratified as her eyes drank in his body, her gaze skimming down his chest to the jut of his erection.

"You're beautiful," she said.

"That's my line."

Nostrils flaring, she reached out to run a finger along the indentations of muscle at his hips. "I don't know what these are called, but they melt my brain. All I can think about is licking them." She bent and did just that, trailing the tip of her tongue along the groove from his hip on down to—

Hudson gently but firmly grabbed her head to keep her from moving further south.

Audrey looked up at him with a faint pout. "Turnabout is fair play."

"Later. When we manage that bed." Not that he thought recovery would be an issue. It seemed he'd been at least semi-erect from the moment they'd met. But he wanted to be inside her the first time he came. With that in mind, he dug his wallet out of his jeans and retrieved the condom.

Audrey snatched it from his hands and ripped it open.

"You first," he said.

"I've already been twice today, and I've pretty much been wet ever since. We go together this time." To end the discussion, she sheathed him.

He lifted her up onto an empty counter, stepping between her thighs and pulling her to the edge. Skimming his hands from her knees to her hips, he searched for some control. This wasn't how he'd imagined their first time. It had been a very long time for her. He'd wanted to give her some romance, some tenderness.

But Audrey wrapped her fingers around his cock, positioning him at her entrance and lifting her mouth to his. "Now. Please, Hudson, I need you inside me now."

He slipped slowly inside her. She was tight, her inner muscles already beginning to ripple around him as he retreated and pressed in again, then again, achingly slow, until he was buried in all that wet heat. Nothing had ever felt more perfect than the grip of her body around him. He held still as she adjusted to him, dragging his focus to her face. Her eyes were closed, her breath held.

Taking a hard grip on his own desire, Hudson lifted a hand to her cheek. "Audrey? You okay?"

Those eyes opened and the blue was almost swallowed by her pupils. "You feel so good," she moaned, hands digging into his shoulders. "More."

As relief surged through him, he took her mouth and began to move. She gave as good as she got, rocking against him until his control hung by a thread.

"Deeper." To emphasize the order, she wrapped her legs around his waist and squeezed.

Surrounded by her body, her scent, her vitality, Hudson lost it. Gripping her hips, he pounded into her, grinding against her clit with every thrust, chasing her fire with fevered intensity, until they were both gasping, groaning, lost to the pleasure. Her head dropped to his shoulder and she bit down to hold in the scream as she broke apart in his arms. The feel of her teeth, the clench of her body, ripped away the last of his control. It dragged him over the edge, until he poured out his own shuddering release.

They stayed that way, still joined, for long minutes, as ragged breathing eased. He came back to himself, registering the feel of her sweat dampened skin stuck to his, the perfect weight of her in his arms. He felt alive for the first time in ages. On the heels of that realization came the barest edge of guilt. He was alive.

At last, Audrey lifted her head and brushed her lips over his. "Oh yeah, we have to find a bed."

Hudson huffed out a laugh with what breath he had left. Which was amazing. She was amazing. And he intended to enjoy that for however much time they had left.

CHAPTER 11

"SOOOOO, YOU GOT IN awfully late last night." Sam's sing-song voice greeted Audrey as she came out of the bathroom, wrapped in a towel.

"So I did," she confirmed, moving across to pull fresh underwear out of her bag.

"And?"

"And what?" Audrey asked, keeping her expression bland. "I was with Hudson."

"Yeah, but were you *with* him?"

Courtesy of the extra backup condom in his wallet, they'd spent quite a while longer exhausting each other before finally stumbling back to their cabins a few hours before dawn. At the memory, a blush heated Audrey's cheeks.

Sam squealed and knelt on her bed, clutching a pillow in her arms. "Oh my God, tell me everything!"

"That's personal."

"Oh, come on! Girl code! Those who are getting lucky must share the delicious details with those who are regrettably single."

"No sparks between you and Charlie?"

"Please. He's like my delightfully playful brother. Actually, my brother's a Navy SEAL, so he's a helluva lot *more* playful. If I wanted to short sheet somebody or make an underwear raid in the middle of the night, Charlie's my man. But he's not a candidate for warming my bed. For now, I must live vicariously through you. Is what's underneath the clothes as impressive as what I imagine?"

Shimmying into a pair of light cargo pants, Audrey gave in. This was one of those female rituals she'd always envied from the outside. How often did she have anything worth sharing? "It's better. His job does amazing things for that body. As to the rest... God was generous with the good genes."

Sam muffled an envious scream in her pillow. "I'm not going to ask if he was good. You're glowing."

Audrey felt amazing. She hadn't even cared that her PT took extra time or that she was feeling sore muscles in places she'd forgotten she had. After they met for a late breakfast, she and Hudson would be putting their heads together to figure out exactly where they could find some privacy to work them out even more. Her vote was for somewhere they could be clothing optional the rest of the week. It seemed a shame to cover up any of that magnificent body of his. She wondered how long a box of condoms would last.

"You two seem to have gotten pretty close since we've been here. Are y'all gonna keep in touch after camp?"

And just like that, her erotic fantasy collapsed. She tugged on a shirt and didn't meet Sam's gaze. "We're adhering to a strict, no talking about the end of camp policy."

"But—"

A brisk knock on the cabin door cut her off.

Not caring who was on the other side, Audrey called out, "Come in."

The door opened and Hudson all but bounded through, the grin on his face almost as bright as the sun slanting through the windows. He crossed the room in two strides and scooped Audrey off her feet, spinning her in a circle and kissing her senseless in a matter of seconds.

When he collapsed back on her bed, cushioning their fall, she gasped out, "Well, good morning to you, too!"

"John moved his hand. Rachel was talking to him yesterday, asking him questions, and he squeezed hers back." The eyes that had been stormy and gray seemed lighter as he smiled up at her.

"That's wonderful!" Audrey didn't know a whole lot about traumatic brain injuries or comas, but she hoped that this was only the first in a long line of victories for his friend. And she hoped it merited the explosion of hope it had inspired in Hudson.

"We're going to celebrate," he announced.

"Well okay then!"

"How do you feel about camping?" He laced his hands behind her back, keeping her sprawled out over the top of him.

As Audrey couldn't find reason to complain about the position, she relaxed. "Like in a tent, packing in all our gear, away from civilization kind of camping?"

"Like shared sleeping bag and all the s'mores you can eat away from civilization kind of camping."

Alone time. Hell yes. "I'm game."

"How fast can you be ready?"

It turned out Audrey could get ready a lot faster than they could gather up the requisite gear from camp. But after lunch they set out with loaded packs and a map of the surrounding area. Camp Firefly Falls had a section set aside for primitive camping, but it wasn't secluded enough for their purposes, so Hudson had arranged for a permit to camp in the national park on the other side of the lake. The hike in took about three hours, as they stopped for frequent breaks. Audrey knew that was for her benefit and appreciated that he didn't seem to resent it. Hudson himself seemed so hyped up, he could've run a marathon, pack and all. By the time he'd decided on a campsite—a lovely copse of trees about fifteen yards from a stream—she was more than ready to get things set up and start dinner.

At his direction, she began assembling the tent poles.

"John, Steve, and I used to do this all the time growing up."

It was the first time he'd mentioned his friends without a shadow of pain. "Yeah? You all grew up in Syracuse, right?"

"Within half a mile of each other. We started out with pup tents in the back yard. Graduated on up to a tree house when we were ten. Then Boy Scouts."

He continued to talk as they put up the tent, telling stories about their adventures. Every word built a picture of rock solid, life-long friendship that was as foreign to Audrey as the dark side of the moon. She wanted that. Ached for it somewhere down deep. It was far too late for her, but she wanted that for her children someday. Children she could suddenly picture with clear gray eyes.

"—but really, all we needed was a sleeping bag, pocket knife, flashlight, water, and peanut butter sandwiches."

Audrey swallowed against a throat gone dry and forced a smile. "I hope we have something with a bit more substance for dinner."

"S'mores, of course. I haven't looked to see what else they packed, but the kitchen staff assured me it was a rustic, romantic dinner for two."

"Romantic, huh?"

He offered a faux casual shrug as he threaded the pole through the loops on the nylon tent. "I might've let slip I wanted to impress a girl."

"You impress me daily."

"I'm about to impress you more. I brought a surprise."

"Oh yeah?" Interested, she watched as he wrestled something out of the bottom of his pack.

"I made a run into town. That's part of why it took so long."

Audrey angled her head to read the side of the box. "You bought us an air mattress?"

"I figured we had plans." He waggled his eyebrows. "Besides, it's not good for you to sleep on the hard ground. I want you to enjoy this trip and be as comfortable as possible. Even if I risk being accused of glamping."

Audrey's heart gave a painful squeeze. He'd gone out of his way—again—to make sure she was taken care of. She knew he didn't think of himself as a hero, and yet he kept proving that he was, day after day, with the big things and the small. He made her feel valued and cherished in a way no one ever had. How could she ever walk away from this man? The hero of her heart.

Because she didn't want to make a big thing out of it, she injected a lightness to her tone as she slid her arms around his shoulder. "I appreciate your willingness to risk your man card on my behalf and will be happy to reward you appropriately later on."

"I definitely like the sound of that. Especially since I haven't even shown you the best feature of this thing."

"What's that?" she asked.

Hudson's lips curved in a wicked grin. "It's self-inflating."

"Thoughtful *and* expedient. I do love a man who can plan." And as he set about unrolling the air mattress and flipping on the blower, Audrey was forced to admit—to herself, at least—that she'd fallen in love with this one.

"IF WE DON'T UNZIP the door, do you suppose we can pretend it isn't morning?" As Audrey's bare shoulder was only a couple of inches from his mouth, Hudson pressed a kiss there.

With a sleepy, satisfied purr, she stretched back against him, then winced.

He propped up on an elbow and looked down at her, worried he'd overdone it. "You okay?"

She grimaced. "I'm afraid I do a very good impersonation of an arthritic octogenarian first thing in the morning. It takes a lot of stretching and PT exercises to get me moving."

"Let me help."

Hudson took it as progress when she only smiled. "First time I've done them naked, with company."

He knew they'd have to pack up and head back to camp soon, but he wasn't in any hurry to leave their private little oasis. And Hudson, Jr. was ever hopeful of one last repeat performance. "I'm a firm believer in positive reinforcement for completing your mandatory PT."

Her eyes sparkled. "I have been known to reward myself with chocolate for breakfast. But we finished that off last night with the s'mores."

"I expect we can come up with a suitable replacement."

A feline smile curved her lips as her gaze dropped to his crotch, where his cock was already stirring again. "Mmm, yes please."

"So polite." Hudson took the leg she offered and followed her instructions for where and how to stretch it. Before releasing it, he dug his fingers into the muscles, massaging the stiffness. Audrey made a sound very close to the moans of pleasure he'd coaxed out of her when they'd made love at dawn.

He'd miss this. He'd miss her. And that had his brain treading perilously close to that whole topic of life outside of camp that they were avoiding. But maybe...maybe they didn't have to. "Why were you in Syracuse?"

Her lashes fluttered back open. "What?"

"Two years ago. Why were you in Syracuse?"

Those blue eyes went sharp on his. "I was driving cross country from Toronto to Yale for a seminar."

"Yale?"

"Mmm. It's where I went to graduate school."

Over the past days, it had been easy to forget she was a girl genius. She didn't talk about work. But Ivy League grad school at *nineteen*. Damn. "What exactly does one do with a Ph.D. in sociology from Yale?"

"Research usually. It's what I was doing before the accident. I wound up in Chattanooga because they offered me a teaching position that I could still manage around my surgeries and physical therapy. Most of my classes are online. But I'm healed up, so it's time for me to rejoin the real world professionally."

"And you'll have to leave Chattanooga to do that?" Hudson kept his voice casual.

"Yeah. The next logical step is taking a tenure track position at a large research university." She paused, beginning to work the other leg. "I interviewed for a position at UC Berkeley right before I came to camp."

"California." It might as well be Australia.

She sighed with an utter lack of enthusiasm that had an unreasonable surge of hope burgeoning in his chest. "Yeah. If they offered me the job, it would be a big feather in my professional cap, get me back on the fast track, almost as if the accident never happened."

"But?" *Please let there be a but.*

"I don't actually like California. They don't have real seasons out there. Not like I'm used to. And…"

Hudson's heart began to pound as he waited for her to continue. When she didn't, he prompted, "And?"

"And—this is practically heresy in my family—I don't know if I still want the things I wanted before the accident. With everything my parents sacrificed for my education, I'm pretty sure they'd have a cow if I walked away from all that. But I've gotten to where I like the slower pace. I'd never have had the time for something like Camp Firefly Falls in a research position. It's all about publish or perish, eighty-hour work weeks, and always pursuing the next grant. I...can't imagine going back to that." She gave a little laugh. "Which is a moot point. They haven't offered me the job, and considering I've been out of mainstream academia for two years, they probably won't."

It sounded like a misery to him. He began to massage her other calf. "What *do* you want?"

She was silent so long, he didn't think she'd answer. "Marriage. Family. A *life*. When I'm ninety, I don't want to be in a place where I've got academic accolades out the wazoo but no one to sit by a fire and read with. If I were in a different discipline and my research held the potential to be life changing, maybe I'd feel differently. But that's not what I do. What I've done. Not that I couldn't change my area of research to something more impactful, but...figuring out the why of things just doesn't seem as important as it used to. And I haven't figured out what to do with that. It's a scary thing finding out that the path you've been certain of your whole life isn't necessarily the right one."

"Did you really pick that path or did your parents kinda shove you on it?"

She considered the question. "Hard to say at this point. I was on board from the beginning. I'd still be on board if not for the accident. I guess, in a way, I'm grateful it happened."

"Really?"

She tugged her leg free and sat up, brushing a quick kiss over his lips. "It brought me you." Her hand slid into the hair at his nape. "However long it lasts, I'm beyond grateful for that."

Emotion tangled in his chest—a bittersweet mix of regret for the brevity of their time and a longing for something he hardly dared hope could be a possibility. She was a gift. A reminder that not all the world was darkness and despair. Hudson laced his hand with hers and brought them to his lips. "I'm grateful for you." For more things than he was prepared to say. So, he laid her back and showed her instead.

Much later, they strolled back into Camp Firefly Falls holding hands like a couple of giddy teenagers.

"Not gonna lie. I'm going to hog every drop of hot water in the shower," Audrey declared.

He hooked an arm around her shoulders as they went up her cabin steps. "You could share. Really, it's the environmentally responsible thing to do."

"You cannot possibly—Can you?"

Hudson shrugged. It seemed worth the ache in his balls to try for the chance to see her naked, wet, and soapy. "Looks like Sam's out. We could hang a sock on the door."

"You're incorrigible." But she grinned as she said it.

The phone in his pocket buzzed as several texts hit at once.

Audrey dumped her pack. "You get that. I'll go start the shower and let the water warm up."

Admiring her very fine backside, Hudson fished out his phone to find two missed calls and several text messages from Rachel. They all had the same theme, with an increasing level of urgency. *Call me.*

He dialed immediately. She picked up on the second ring.

"Rach? I've been out of cell range. What's up?"

"Hud, I…" At the strain in her voice, his hand tightened on the phone.

"Rachel?"

"John's gone, Hud."

The denial was swift and automatic. "No. No. You said he was getting better. He squeezed your hand."

Audrey came out of the bathroom, her hand covering her mouth.

On the phone, Rachel was still talking, her tone choked. "The doctors warned us this was a possibility in the beginning. A probability."

"No," Hudson snarled. "There are things they could have done, kept him going until he could get better."

"Hudson." Rachel's voice was gentle. "You know how he felt about life support. He didn't want to be hooked up to machines, and he filed a do not resuscitate order."

In some dim, distant part of his brain, Hudson recognized that he was out of line. That taking his grief out on John's widow was beyond a dick thing to do. But that realization was drowned out by the grief that battered him like hail.

John was dead.

Yesterday, he'd been alive. He'd been alive and responsive for the first time in three months. And instead of getting in his Jeep and driving home, Hudson had taken that news as a sign from God that he could let go and live again himself. That his friend was on the mend. That they'd have more time. He'd missed Rachel's messages. And he'd missed his chance to say goodbye.

CHAPTER 12

*A*UDREY'S HEART CRACKED RIGHT in two as Hudson stood there, broad shoulders rigid, hand white knuckling the phone. It was obvious that his celebration yesterday had been premature, and the worst had come to pass. Tears clogged her own throat on his behalf. This would break him in a way nothing else could.

"Did he ever wake up?" The voice that had been full of fun and laughter just minutes before now trembled.

His shoulders slumped at Rachel's answer. For a few more minutes, he listened, grunting monosyllabic responses as a muscle jumped in his jaw. "I'll be there."

As soon as he hung up the phone, Audrey crossed the room. She wasn't even sure he saw her. But she slid her arms around him anyway, needing to do anything she could to comfort him. "I'm so sorry."

He stood rigid, his breath ragged. She held him tighter, willing him to take what she offered. At long last, he wrapped around her, burying his face in her hair. He began to shake, the force of the emotions he was holding back almost too great to bear. Audrey wanted to tell him to just let go, that he didn't have to be strong with her, that he could grieve. But she didn't know how he'd respond. Instead she stroked his back, hoping the fact that he wasn't alone was, at least, a little bit of comfort.

"I'm going home." His voice was muffled, thick with emotion.

"Of course, you are." He'd hardly stay at camp after this. The funeral would probably be in a few days. "When?"

He pulled away. "Today. Now."

Even expecting it, Audrey couldn't stop the visceral rejection of that. No. She'd just found him. She wasn't ready to let him go. But she swallowed back the protests. This wasn't about her. "Okay. I'll help you pack."

Recognizing that he needed to move, she towed him toward the door. Hudson dropped her hand to scoop up his pack and followed. They didn't speak on the walk to his cabin. Nor did they touch. With every step, she could feel him retreating from her, and she didn't know what to do about it.

Charlie wasn't at the cabin, and she was grateful to have a little while longer alone with Hudson. They went through the motions, gathering up his stuff. When he would have just shoved it all into his bags, she stopped to fold things, wanting to delay his departure and not at all sure he was in any shape to drive. She didn't dare ask if he was okay. He clearly wasn't.

"Maybe you should wait a little bit, until you've had some time to process this, before you get behind the wheel."

The gaze he turned on her was flat, a desolate nothing that was worse than anger or pain. "They're waiting for me. I need to go."

He needed to run. To escape. Desperation was clear in every staccato movement. He was barely holding it together, and Audrey was terrified of what might happen when he really broke.

"I could come with you." The words were out before she could think better of them. It was too soon, too intimate. A thing you offered when you were in a true relationship, and they were... Audrey didn't know what they were. But they'd shared more than just fun and laughter this week. More than sex. That had to count for something.

"What?"

"I could go back to Syracuse with you."

"Why?"

His tone was so baffled, she regretted making the offer. But she'd already started down this path, so she pushed on. "For you. To be a support. To help. Whatever you need."

For the first time since they'd met, Hudson stared at her like the freak she'd so often felt like. The strange one. The out-of-sync. And she knew she'd said the wrong thing.

"This is my real life, Audrey. The real world. Whatever we've had, whatever this has been, ends at the camp property line. We agreed on that."

No, they'd agreed not to talk about it. Maybe an ending had been implicit, but she'd thought, after last night—

"There's no room for this where I'm going. You're a distraction I can't afford."

He was grieving, angry at the world and blaming himself. She was the nearest target. But even seeing that, knowing it, didn't diminish the pain of his words. How could he reduce what they'd shared to a mere distraction?

Audrey knit her hands and hated herself for the show of weakness. She had to work at keeping her voice steady. "You've helped me through so much. I just wanted to return the favor."

"I appreciate the thought, but I don't need help."

"Everybody needs help sometimes. There's no shame in that."

"And what help would you be, exactly? You need rescuing every time you turn around. I can't be that guy. Especially not now. I've got too much on my plate."

She flinched away as if he'd struck her. "I didn't ask you to rescue me," she whispered. "I didn't ask for any of this."

"Neither did I." He tossed his duffel bags over his shoulder. "Goodbye, Audrey." And without another word, he walked out.

She sank down on his bed, her knees knocking together too hard to continue to stand. She was still sitting there some time later when Charlie and Sam came into the cabin, laughing and joking.

"Audrey! You're back! How did the great camping trip go?" Sam asked.

"Hey, where's Hudson's stuff?" Charlie asked.

Audrey raised her head to look at them, her whole body feeling leaden from her own grief. "Gone," she managed and burst into tears.

"Firefighter John Matthew McCleary—Lehigh County Dispatch."

The sound of the radio was too loud over the sober masses by the graveside. It raked Hudson's already raw nerves and made him want to scream. The waiting silence as the dispatcher began John's last call was worse.

"Firefighter John Matthew McCleary—Lehigh County Dispatch."

Hud's hands curled to fists as he stared at the flag-draped coffin on the little dais beneath the tent. He wanted to think his heart couldn't break any further, but every moment of this funeral shattered it just a little more.

"Having heard no response, we know that Firefighter McCleary has responded to his last call on Earth and that the fire department in the hereafter has a new responder."

A soft, choked noise came from Rachel as the dispatcher continued.

"Firefighter McCleary served the citizens of Lehigh County for twelve years. We appreciate Firefighter McCleary's dedication and his family's sacrifices during the time he was a Firefighter. Your warm laugh and ready smile will be missed." The dispatcher's voice hitched for a moment before she continued. "Firefighter McCleary, you have now become a Guardian who will help watch out for all Firefighters as they respond to emergencies. You've completed your tour as a Firefighter in this life and are clear to remain with the Lord forever. Goodbye, and we'll take it from here."

The dispatcher signed off, advising all units of a moment of silence.

When it was done, the bugler, set up on a hill about twenty-five yards away, began to play TAPS. Hudson stepped toward the casket, along with another of the honor guard, and began to fold the flag. It was a ritual he'd performed just months ago for Steve. He'd barely held it together for Steve's mom. The fresh pain of John's death all but took him to his knees as his hands performed their duty. He clenched his teeth, forcing himself to hold on to his emotions for Rachel's sake. Per ceremony, he turned to present the flag to the fire chief, who turned and knelt, presenting it to Rachel. John's widow, who would never again hear her husband laugh or make jokes, would never bear his children, or grow old by his side. In unrelieved black and the pearls John had given her for their fifth anniversary, she clutched the flag, lifting her eyes to Hudson's.

God, how could she even look at him?

Shame that he was the reason for this clogged his throat. But he didn't look away. He owed Rachel that much. They held each other's gaze, lost in shared grief, until Hudson realized the other mourners were filing away. The funeral was over. Everything was over. And he didn't have the first clue how to go on living. He moved to Rachel, wanting to offer—what? His condolences? His service? His life? The wish that he could trade places with John and give them the long life together they'd deserved? Nothing would ever be enough to make up for John's sacrifice.

"Rach, I—" What could he say? In the end, he said nothing, wrapping his arms around her. As she rested her head against his chest, the flag trapped between them, he looked away, searching the crowds for some kind of an answer, some sort of guidance.

A flash of red hair had him going stock still, his heart shooting into his throat. But the woman walking away from the graveside had too even a gait in the three-inch heels and none of the scars crisscrossing the legs that were bare beneath the black funeral dress. Not Audrey. Of course, it wouldn't be Audrey. He'd made it perfectly, painfully clear where they stood that last day at camp. Nowhere.

It had to be that way. When she'd made her offer, every cell in his body had wanted to grab her up and fall to his knees in thanks that she was willing to endure this with him. And he didn't deserve that kindness. He didn't deserve any sort of a buffer against the grief and guilt. How could he possibly have accepted her offer of support, when Rachel was here with no one? Never mind the friends and family who'd turned out, lining the streets of town. She was alone because of him, and Hudson couldn't even think of moving on with his own life now.

So, he'd lashed out, striking at her in the only way that would ensure she'd stay at camp and not do something crazy like come up to Syracuse on her own. In his way, he'd meant it. There was no room for her in the life he had here. Because eventually her sweet nature and enthusiasm for the second chance she'd been given would heal him—which he didn't deserve. Or those same things he loved about her would dim. Her light would go out in the face of the toxic shit that was his world right now—and she deserved better than that. So, he'd been cruel, saving her one last time, this time from him.

No, Audrey wouldn't be coming back into his life. But he realized, as he stared at the retreating back of the other woman, that a part of him had been looking for her anyway.

"Hud? What is it?" Rachel was following his gaze.

He shook himself. "It's nothing."

She'd be expected back at the house for the reception. It would be overflowing with family, friends, other first responders. He dreaded the whole thing and couldn't imagine how she was bearing up so well under the strain. But he'd be there. He'd do whatever could be done to lighten her load. He'd take care of her in John's absence.

With a sigh, he steeled himself. "Are you ready?" The moment the words were out, he wished he could take them back. Was anyone ever ready to face the endless sympathy and parade of casseroles that hammered home the death of a loved one?

Rachel kissed her fingers, then laid them over the polished wood of the coffin. The finality of the gesture gutted him. Then she straightened her shoulders and took the arm he offered. "Let's go honor my husband."

CHAPTER 13

"THEY'RE SETTING UP FOR the talent show in the lodge. You should come." Sam's voice was overly cheerful, as if by sheer will alone she could counter Audrey's melancholy.

Audrey glanced up at her from her potter's wheel and didn't move, her hands still wrapped around the rhythmic turning of the clay. "I'm fine here."

"Honey, you've been holed up in here for days. We're going home day after tomorrow. I don't want to see you skipping out on the last of camp."

Audrey would've happily gone home as soon as Hudson left. If Sam hadn't been with her, she would have. But they'd paid for the full two weeks and Sam was having a blast, so she'd stayed. Everything at Camp Firefly Falls reminded her of Hudson and made her ache—being here in the pottery studio especially. But she'd found it soothing before him, and she'd be damned if he'd ruin that for her, too. So, she'd stayed hidden, avoiding the other campers, and counting down the days until she could leave.

"I'm itching to get back to work." Which was a partial truth.

She was itching to get back to the university, to a world that made sense to her, where she knew the expectations.

Sam knit her hands, her brow furrowed with distress. "Audrey."

"I'm fine."

"You're not. You're barely eating. You're not sleeping. I'm worried about you."

Audrey sighed. She'd appreciate the friendship later, but right now, she just wanted to be alone in her misery. "Okay, I'm not. But I'll *be* fine when we get home." Where she wouldn't think of Hudson everywhere she turned.

"I'm sorry I pushed you into pursuing him."

"You didn't push me into anything I wasn't gunning for myself. And you hardly pushed me into bed with him. I made that decision on my own." Because it hadn't been simple attraction pulling them together. They'd found something with each other. Something she'd come to treasure. She just...hadn't expected he'd let it go so easily.

"Are you in love with him?" Sam asked quietly.

Audrey dropped her head, wishing her hair was loose instead of gathered in a knot at her nape, so she could hide from the question. Because she'd known the answer when they'd gone camping, and she didn't want to think about the truth of it.

"I think...I've been a little bit in love with a fantasy version of him since he pulled me out of that car. But the time with him here? Getting to know the real man? That just blew the fantasy out of the water."

Sam laid a hand on Audrey's shoulder. "I'm so sorry he hurt you."

"He didn't do it deliberately." Audrey was rational enough to recognize that. He was drowning in grief and guilt and shoving her away because he didn't believe he deserved anything good in his life. Not that what he'd said stung any less. "And he never made me any promises. I was the one who tried to change the rules." Because she cared about him, and she was worried about how he was coping with John's death. She was still worried. Not that she'd heard from him. He was well and truly out of her life. It was on her to learn how to live with that.

The outside door to the building opened. Audrey hoped someone else was coming to work in the studio and that it would put a stop to Sam's well-intentioned attempts to talk about this.

Heather stepped into the room. "Hey Audrey. I was hoping I'd find you here. You've got a phone call up at the lodge."

Audrey's fingers flexed, and the wall of her vase dipped in, the whole thing collapsing. "Who is it?"

"I don't know, but he was very insistent that he talk to you. He's still on hold."

Hudson. A surge of hope had her fumbling to turn off the wheel. She dumped the entire failed vase into the scrap bucket, quickly washing her hands. "Lead the way."

Was the funeral over? Had he realized he needed her? Did he regret what he'd said? Maybe he just wanted to apologize. The possibilities rolled around in her head like a bag of spilled marbles, shooting off in all directions. By the time they made it to the lodge office, her heart was tripping double time.

"I'll just give you some privacy." Heather shut the door behind her.

Audrey scooped up the receiver. "Hello, this is Audrey."

"Dr. Graham! This is Dr. Feinstein out at UC Berkeley."

Surprise was quickly chased by disappointment. Of course, it wouldn't be Hudson. Why should anything have changed with him? He'd made his position perfectly clear.

She struggled to keep her tone professional. "Sir. How unexpected to hear from you."

"Yes, I apologize for bothering you on your vacation. I got the number from your parents. It's just that the board has made a decision, and I didn't want to wait to get in touch with you. We're delighted to offer you a position on our faculty."

Shock stole her voice for a long moment. She hadn't even thought about Berkeley since she got to camp, other than briefly mentioning the interview to Hudson, and here the department head was offering Audrey her textbook perfect job on a platter.

Her brain kicked in. *Say something.* "I...wow. I'm so flattered." She ought to be beyond flattered. This was what she'd been waiting for, a chance to get back to the academic fast track and make up for lost time. No one could have predicted that they'd jump at her with the two-year gap in research.

"I'm sure you're entertaining multiple offers, and we wanted to get in at the front of the pack."

She listened as Dr. Feinstein continued to talk about the details of the offer, making notes and asking questions, re-engaging the academic side of her brain. And it was good to feel wanted, mollifying to feel respected. This was her world. The place where she was most comfortable. As the conversation continued, she found herself getting excited about academia again. The position would be a challenge. She hadn't had a real mental challenge, something she could sink her teeth into, since before the accident.

Well, she'd had Hudson. She'd felt...needed and useful trying to help him embrace life again. But she'd failed him in the end. He wouldn't take his second chance at life. But maybe she could explore that area in formal research. It was something to consider.

"I still need some time to think about it before I give a final answer."

"Of course. Of course." Dr. Feinstein was all agreeableness. "We look forward to hearing from you and hope you'll be joining our faculty this fall."

As Audrey told him goodbye and hung up, she considered that maybe this was exactly the sign she'd been waiting for.

HUDSON SHUT the door to Rachel's house after the last guest. "I'm glad that's over."

From her position on the sofa, Rachel kicked off her pumps and flexed her feet. "It was good, though. To hear all the stories."

"John was well loved." Hudson crossed back to the living room, slipping off his dress uniform coat and draping it over a chair. "Want a drink?"

"God, yes. There's wine in the kitchen."

He poured her a glass, then cracked open the fridge to grab a beer. But there wasn't one. Because Rachel didn't drink beer, and John hadn't lived here in three months. Wishing for something stronger now, he splashed some more of the wine into a second glass for himself and went back to join Rachel on the sofa.

"I'm glad everybody shared their pictures." She took the wine and continued to scroll through image after image on her laptop. John at picnics or family functions. John around town. Some were of John at work, cleaning or storing equipment or otherwise horsing around the firehouse. Steve was in so many, and so was Hudson. They'd both been an inextricable part of his life, and without them, it felt like everything was unraveling.

"Have you added yours?" she asked.

"Not sure what all I've got." Hudson pulled out his phone and unlocked it before handing it over to Rachel. He took a testing sip of the wine. Not his preference, but it didn't totally suck.

Rachel had paused on some picture or other, an odd expression on her face.

"What is it?" he asked. Man, had one of the guys taken some kind of compromising picture he didn't know about? Maybe he should've pre-screened what was on there.

She turned the phone around. "Who is she?"

From the screen a familiar, smiling face stared out, pressed cheek-to-cheek with his. Hud felt a stab of pain at the sight of it. "Audrey."

Rachel rolled her eyes. "Which tells me next to nothing. Who is she *to you?* A woman you met at camp?"

He took a bigger gulp of wine. "Not exactly. I worked an accident she was in a couple years ago." He told her about the wreck and how Audrey had ended up at Camp Firefly Falls.

"Wow. That seems like kismet."

Of course, Rachel, with her gooshy, romantic heart, would think that. "It's just a small world."

"You spent a lot of time with her?"

Only every waking minute. "A fair bit."

"You're smiling in this picture."

Hud knew she was fishing. Under other circumstances he'd have shut this line of questioning down fast. But this was as much about distraction for her as interest in what had been going on with him. "Yeah. It was a good day." She'd made him take basket weaving with her. The corner of his mouth quirked as he remembered her excitement.

"I never thought I'd see that."

He drained the wine and shrugged. "Haven't had a lot of cause for smiling since the accident."

"It's not even that. I've known you since we were in diapers, and I've *never* seen you smile like this, Hud."

There was no good answer to that.

She laid a hand on his arm. "I'm sorry the timing worked out like this and we had to call you home."

Covering her hand with his was automatic. "It's fine." It was probably for the best. He'd gotten in over his head. Another few days with her and he might've started considering something drastic, and that was just crazy. His family, his duty, were here.

"When are you going to see her again?"

There went that pang again. He'd give almost anything for another chance to hold her, to hear her laugh. But that wasn't gonna happen. He'd made sure of that. "I'm not."

"What do you mean you're not?"

"I mean today's the last day of camp. Everybody goes home tomorrow. She lives in Tennessee." Or she'd be moving to California or Timbuktu. Somewhere that was far, far away from him. And after how he'd treated her, Hudson couldn't blame her.

"So? There's this thing called a phone and modern transportation."

"Chattanooga isn't exactly a hop, skip, and a jump, Rach. And I don't have any of her contact information. Besides all that, she's not going to want to see me again."

"Why not? It looks like she adores you. And that the feeling is mutual."

"We didn't exactly part on great terms."

Rachel frowned. "Did she have some problem with you leaving early?"

"She offered to come with me." How many times in the past few days had he wished he'd taken her up on that offer? How many times had he wanted to reach for her, to feel her arms around him in that calm, quiet way she had?

"Why didn't she?"

Hudson didn't want to talk about this anymore. He started to rise, but Rachel tightened her grip on his arm.

"Why didn't she come, Hud?"

"Because I shot her down." Even as he'd done it, he'd felt like such an asshole.

"Why?"

"Because you don't bring a woman you've known less than two weeks to your best friend's funeral. And you sure as hell don't flaunt her in front of his widow." He shoved up and began to pace. "I had to shut things down. Things were getting too serious, and I can't do serious." Even if he could, he'd destroyed her trust in him, left her bleeding.

Rachel stared at him, mouth agape. "What the hell is wrong with you?"

"Excuse me?"

"You can't do serious? Hudson, you're one of the most committed people I know."

"It doesn't change anything. My commitment has to be here. To you, to the family, to my company."

"This isn't about me or your family or the company. The only thing you're committed to is acting like you never got pulled out of that fire."

Hudson stopped dead. "Excuse me?"

"I get that you're grieving. That's natural and proper. But John did not haul your ass out of that burning building so that you could curl up and pretend you died anyway. He hauled you out because he loved you. So you would live. This whole retreat from the world and everything good in it routine you've had going since the fire is an insult to John and a disservice to everything he stood for. He gave you a second chance at life. How dare you do anything but use it?"

"Use it? What? I'm supposed to just go on, every day, like John's death isn't *my fault?*"

"Yes, damn it. Because it wasn't your fault."

"He died because he came after me. I don't know how you can even look at me."

"If he hadn't gone after you, he wouldn't have been the man I loved from the time I was fourteen. He believed in the job, and I believed in him. We knew the risks. And yes, I lost the love of my life. But I don't blame you for it. You need to stop blaming yourself."

Hudson didn't know what that looked like and couldn't understand how she could even think it. "How can you be so calm about this? We just put your husband in the ground this morning."

"Because I lost him three months ago. I knew it. The doctors knew it. Everyone knew it but you. You were the only one who expected he'd wake up."

"You just gave up?"

"No. I hoped and prayed every day. But he couldn't come back from that, and it was time for him to let go." She came to him, wrapping her arms around him in a tight hug. "Now it's your turn. You have to let go of this half-life, Hud. You have to honor him by living."

He buried his face in her hair, barely able to speak past the pain in his chest. "I don't know how."

Rachel pulled back to look into his face. "I think you know someone who can teach you."

Wasn't that what Audrey had been doing the entire time at camp? Encouraging him to embrace life again? He'd done it for her. Now it was time to do it for himself.

Even as he thought it, he remembered the look of devastation on her face. All that time spent protecting her from every imagined danger, and he'd deliberately, callously, hit her where he knew it would hurt the most. The back of Hudson's neck got hot. "I was an asshole when I left."

"So, get your ass on the road and go apologize. You have one more night to make it right. Go make the most of it."

Hudson didn't know if he could make it right. He didn't know if she'd ever want to see him again. But he had to go and try to repair the damage he'd done to her and set the record straight.

CHAPTER 14

"*I*T IS THE LAST night of camp. You are not spending it holed up in our cabin or the pottery studio." Hands on hips, Sam glared at Audrey. "So, get dressed. Or don't. I don't actually care. But you're going to that dance tonight if I have to get Charlie to toss you over his shoulder."

Audrey just arched a brow. "You'd really haul me to the boathouse in my bathrobe?"

"In a New York minute."

Audrey knew she was just crazy enough to do it.

Sam flopped down on the bed. "Honey, I know this whole trip didn't turn out like you wanted, but you can't let your last memory of camp be of moping around."

Audrey wanted to protest that she hadn't been moping, but it would've been a lie. The truth was, all hurt aside, she missed Hudson. And she was worried about how he was coping with his friend's death. Which was wasted emotion. He wasn't a part of her life. Not in any permanent way. That was something she'd come to understand about camp flings—they were intense and glorious because of their brevity.

Would things have been the same between them if there'd been no expiration date? If they'd just met again under circumstances where they could've taken their time, would their attraction still have happened? Or was it just the enforced proximity here at camp that had pulled him into her orbit? Given the hard-core case of survivor's guilt he had going, she might have had the chance to give her thanks, but that would've been it. And she'd have been the poorer for it.

"Please come tonight. At least for a little while."

Audrey didn't want to go. Being around all those happy people, all that noise and boisterous enthusiasm made her want to burrow under the covers and sleep until morning, when they'd be boarding the bus to head back to New York and the airport. But given her luck, their companions on the bus would quiz her about who she was and why she'd been a hermit during camp. Or, worse, ask her what happened with the hottie firefighter who'd saved her ass from death by campfire that first week. Besides, she knew she'd dampened Sam's own pleasure in the whole camp experience, and that really wasn't fair. She'd used up her quota of lousy friend passes.

"Okay. But if I'm going, then it's not going to be in my bathrobe."

Sam grinned and gave a victory fist pump. "Damn straight. If you're going, you might as well knock some socks off. Please let me do your hair and makeup."

Audrey arched a brow. "Are you about to be channeling your Miss Eden's Ridge pageant days?"

"Hush your mouth. I never did pageants. And anyway, didn't you watch *Miss Congeniality?* They're scholarship programs." Sam rummaged around in her stuff and came up with at least four bottles of hair product and a curling iron.

Audrey held up a hand. "I draw the line at hair tall enough to commune with God."

"Noted. Now go get in the shower."

She took her time, as much to let the hot water beat on her

stiff muscles as to procrastinate facing the full contingent of beautification tools at Sam's disposal. By the time she strode out, pleasantly pruney, Sam had a whole station set up. With the panache of a game show host, she waved Audrey to her seat.

"Sit and let me work my magic."

Because it obviously made her friend happy to play stylist, Audrey sat.

"I'm having potentially life-altering thoughts."

Sam's hands paused, roller in hand. "About Hudson?"

"Because of him. About my career, my research."

"I thought you didn't want to do research anymore."

"I didn't know what I wanted to do before. But I'm considering a change in focus. I want to start researching survivor guilt I couldn't help Hudson with his, but maybe I could discover something in my work that could help others like him."

Sam didn't stop moving. "Can't do that in Chattanooga. So, you've decided to take the job in Berkeley?"

"It's an amazing opportunity. The resources I'd have there are unparalleled. It's got me really excited about getting back to my work." She supposed she owed Hudson for that. It wasn't what she'd wanted from him, but as a consolation prize, at least it was an opportunity to do something with true meaning. She needed that in her life now, more than ever.

"I think it's a good idea. But is Berkeley going to go for it?"

"I'm flying out to discuss it with Dr. Feinstein almost as soon as we get home."

"Well, I wish you luck. Even though I'm going to miss you like crazy."

Audrey reached back to lay a hand on Sam's arm. "I'm going to miss you, too. I'll keep in touch."

"Damn straight. Now be still while I finish this."

Her hair was dried, smoothed, then set in loose waves.

"Hate to tell you, but that's going to fall out within five minutes of me stepping outside. My hair doesn't hold curl."

"With this much product, I could get a two-by-four to curl. Now sit still while I do your makeup."

Like an obedient Barbie, Audrey didn't move while Sam swiped, blended, brushed, accented and slicked. "Am I gonna look like a madam when you're done with me?"

"You're going to look like you, just...more." She finished with one more coat of mascara. "There! Take a look at that."

Audrey was glad she had to go into the bathroom for a mirror. It would give her time to put her poker face on before coming back out. But the face that stared back at her wasn't that of a two-bit movie streetwalker. It was, as Sam had said, just her. Except her eyes were bigger, deeper and her cheekbones popped in a way that gave her face a subtle depth. Her lips were glossed a kissable pink. Not that anybody would be taking advantage of that. Still, she couldn't help but be impressed.

"Wow. You're really good at this."

"I'm Southern. We're trained in proper hair and makeup from the time we're knee-high. Plus, my mama owns a salon. Now come back out and let's pick your outfit."

"There's not a lot to pick *from*. I've been in jeans and cargo pants all week."

"All the more reason to wear this." Sam pulled a dress from her bag. Sleeveless, with a V-neck, it was deep blue, made of that stretchy stuff that never wrinkled. "You would look amazing in this."

She would show her legs in that. The skirt would hit her just below the knees. But Audrey's knee-jerk refusal stalled some-where on the tip of her tongue as she thought about Hudson's ease with her scars. He'd never made a thing of them, never made her feel like a freak show. They were simply part of her. If he could accept that, maybe she could, too. Besides, the boat house would be pretty dim lighting.

"Oh, why not?"

By the time Charlie showed up half an hour later, Audrey had managed to unearth a little enthusiasm for the prospect of a dance. Courtesy of Sam's ministrations, she *did* look good—a fact which Charlie underscored with mimed heart palpitations at the sight of her.

"Hubba hubba!"

Audrey laughed. "You are incorrigible."

"What I am is a lucky bastard to have two beautiful ladies to escort tonight." He crooked both his arms. "Shall we?"

Audrey and Sam slid their arms through his.

Audrey stood on her tiptoes and pressed a kiss to his cheek. "Thanks for being a good friend, Charlie."

He covered her hand with his. "Anytime, beautiful. Let's go paint the camp red!"

THE DANCE HAD ALREADY STARTED by the time Hudson rolled back into Camp Firefly Falls. He could hear faint strains of the music thumping as he got out of his Jeep. Would Audrey be there, observing people or would she be off on her own somewhere, away from all the noise? She'd been all about the classic camp experience, and likely everyone was at the boathouse tonight. He trudged in that direction, with no better idea of what he'd say to make things right than he'd had when he left Syracuse two hours before. He'd had plenty of time to replay the scene in his cabin and realize exactly how badly he'd fucked up. He wasn't sure there was an apology big enough to make up for that, but he was sure as hell gonna try.

As it had that first night, the boathouse was jumping. Michael Tully was tending bar again. Though he viciously wanted a beer, Hudson bypassed Michael and wove his way around the edges of the crowd, looking for a familiar flash of red hair. He didn't find her on the first pass. Surely, she hadn't left camp early just because he'd been a dick. God, he hoped he hadn't ruined that for her, too.

He started to head to the pottery studio but took one last look out on the dance floor. And there she was, dancing with Charlie and Sam.

She was wearing a dress. And damn, she was a total knockout with her hair and makeup all done up. He knew what it meant for her to show her legs, and for a moment, he was overcome with a fierce pride that she'd done it. It was different to see her all dressed up instead of in the casual camp clothes she'd worn the last couple of weeks—one of the many sides of her he hoped like hell he'd get a chance to see again after tonight.

Locked in on his target, Hudson wove his way through the dancing crowd, rehearsing his apology. He hadn't gotten much past the basic, *I'm sorry* before she caught sight of him. For a fleeting second, she lit up with pleasure, but by the time he made it to her, she'd locked down that reaction. Not a great reception, but the momentary light gave him hope.

"Hi." *Brilliant opening, Lowell.*

For once, Charlie didn't insert himself into the conversation. He just nodded before he and Sam dropped back, presumably to give them some privacy. But the pair of them stayed close.

Audrey crossed her arms over her middle, her posture half-protective, half-defensive. "You came back."

"Yeah. I had to see you."

Over the sound system, Journey rolled into Thomas Rhett's "Die A Happy Man." Appropriate, if she'd forgive him. Hudson held out a hand. "Can I speak to you? Privately."

She hesitated only a second before placing her hand in his. Sam took a step forward, but Charlie put a restraining hand on her arm. Audrey looked to her friend and gave a tiny shake of her head. Message received. Audrey still trusted him, at least a little. Sam clearly did not.

He wanted to wrap around Audrey, bury his face in her hair, and just hold her until his world righted again. But he'd walked away from the right to do that. So, Hudson led her outside to the pier instead. It seemed appropriate to have this conversation here, where it had all started. She'd been so hesitant that first time he saw her, when she'd followed him outside from the dance—so unsure of her reception. She wasn't hesitant now. Her stride was confident, her back straight. This time he was the one who was uncertain.

Except, no, he realized. That hadn't been the first time he saw her. He'd seen her across the lake that first afternoon. Even from that distance, he'd felt her sense of absolute peace. Envied it. He'd had that with her, for a time, and then he'd destroyed everything.

"I'm sorry." He blurted it out, even knowing he was getting ahead of himself. "I know that doesn't even begin to cover it. I was an asshole, and I hurt you."

"Hudson, I get it. You were grieving."

He didn't deserve the understanding he saw in her face. "Don't make excuses for me. There is no excuse for how I treated you. We both know why I did it, but I have to say it anyway." He had to get this right. Had to fix what he'd broken. "You are the most compassionate person I have ever met. You completely over-looked the fact that I'm a surly, miserable bastard, and did every-thing you could to pull me out of the pit I'd fallen into. And you did it. You brought me back to life in a very real way. Then John died, and I just lost my shit."

"It's okay. Really, I accept your apology."

"No. No, it's not okay. You offered yourself up to help me, to support me, and I hit at you in the worst possible way. It's not true. You *don't* need rescuing all the time. You've been rescuing yourself perfectly well without me." Hudson could feel himself losing control, hear the edge of it in his voice. Because he realized, standing here, seeing her again, exactly what it was he'd thrown away. He loved this woman, with her gigantic heart and fearless determination.

He wanted to reach for her but didn't dare. Everything in him felt taut as a bowstring, ready to snap in two. He'd lost Steve. He'd lost John. Hudson didn't think he could bear losing Audrey, too.

"The truth is, I'm the one who needed saving. I've been drowning. And I had to push you away because I wanted what you were offering so damned badly that if you didn't back off, I was going to hold on and never let go."

Audrey lost that carefully neutral expression, her eyes glimmering in the moonlight. "Hudson." She stepped into him, wrapping her arms tight around his waist.

Thank God. Thank God.

He drew her against him, feeling something deep inside quiet as her body settled against his. He did wrap around her now, pressing his face to her hair, inhaling her scent, feeling the thud of her heart against his. Right and perfect. It felt like coming home.

As they stood in the quiet night, the sounds of the party a world away, Audrey held him and stroked his spine. It was impossible not to think about the first time she'd seen him here—embraced him here—so aloof, holding himself back from life, from connection. An island unto himself. Every step of drawing him out had been a journey of discovery. And the real man had been so much more than her fantasies. Before the call about John, he'd been a changed man, still caring and protective, but also fun and alive. Vibrant. This Hudson was something else again. He was hollow and wounded, and it was breaking her heart.

"I'm sorry. I'm so goddamned sorry."

The remorse in his voice was so hard to hear. He hated himself for the things he'd said far more than she ever had—ever could—and that hurt her. God, he was so brittle. But he'd come back to her.

His words played over in her head.

I wanted what you were offering so damned badly that if you didn't back off, I was going to hold on and never let go.

She didn't want him to let go. Relief and elation burned away the misery of the past days, wiped out everything but the need to comfort him. So, Audrey held on and lifted her mouth to his.

He kissed her like a drowning man chasing a last breath of oxygen. His desperation, his fierceness, rocked her. She gave him everything she had, pouring out all the worry, all the tenderness she felt, until the tension slowly leeched out of him.

Breath not altogether steady, Audrey stood, her brow pressed to his. *I love you.* The words beat against her breast, desperate to get out, but she held them back. It was too soon, too...something. She'd pressed too fast before and he'd bolted. Instead, she said, "God, I missed you."

"I missed you, too. More than I ever imagined. I'd have come back sooner but the funeral was today." There was no mistaking the thread of pain underscoring his words.

She wanted to ask how it had gone, but that felt wrong, too. How did any funeral ever go? In any event, he'd survived it and come back to camp. For her. "I've been worried about you."

"The whole time, I kept wishing you were there, wishing I'd said yes." He cupped her face, rubbing a thumb along her cheek "I wanted to call, but I—I never dreamed you'd forgive me."

"Of course, I forgive you. I'd never hold your grief against you."

Hudson stepped back, running his hands from her shoulders down her arms to take both her hands in his. "I know we said we wouldn't talk about the end of camp. But I need to know you'll give me another chance. A chance for something beyond camp, beyond these two weeks. A chance for something real."

Beyond camp.

Reality came crashing back down on Audrey. Tomorrow it was back to the real world. The real world she'd made plans for without him. Plans that would take her to the other side of the country.

He rolled on, coming as near to babbling as she'd ever heard. "I know it's fast. I know it's crazy. But it was crazy that we found each other in the first place, crazy that we both came here. And I can't just walk away after two weeks. It's not enough."

Her tongue wouldn't work. Here he was offering her everything she'd been dreaming of since she'd met him—or at least the possibility of it. She wanted to take the leap, to grab on to this—to him—with both hands and not let go. And yet...

"Audrey?"

She hadn't answered him.

"I got the job at Berkeley." She said it automatically, because it impacted them, and he needed to know. But she knew at once that absolutely was not what he needed to hear right now.

Hudson pulled back. "Oh."

"I haven't accepted yet." She rushed to say it, wishing she could reel the conversation back a few clicks and take back her announcement, at least until she had a chance to think about the details, the ramifications.

"But you're planning to." It wasn't a question.

"I was. I'm supposed to fly back to California next week to meet with the department chair." But she'd made the plans without him in the equation. She'd had no idea he would come back, no idea he would want to pursue things with her beyond camp.

"Congratulations." Somehow, he managed to dig up a whisper of a smile, though his eyes were dark, devastated. It was like watching everything she'd built with him over the past weeks crumble.

"I can push it back. Take some more time for us to talk about this." She was a fucking prodigy. Surely, she could come up with a way to make this work. "Maybe we can—"

"No." There was no anger in his voice. Just a heart-wrenching resignation. "No, I think this is a sign." He reached out to skim a hand over her cheek. "I'm grateful I got the chance to know you."

Don't do this. Don't close this door.

But Audrey couldn't see an alternative. She *wanted* to get back to her career, needed to get back to a true mental challenge. That had been sorely missing in her life since the accident, and the prospect of having it back wasn't something she could walk away from. Even if money were no object, maintaining a long-distance relationship from one coast almost to the other was madness. She couldn't ask him to leave his family, his friends, his life for the prospect of what might be between them. There was nothing she could say to give them any hope, and they both knew it.

Hudson held out his hand. "I want to dance with you."

Heart squeezing, Audrey took it. They went back to the boathouse, back to the noise and the people. As they stepped onto the dance floor the music rolled into "The Time of My Life" from *Dirty Dancing*. How bittersweet and apropos. So many romantics watched that movie, convinced that Baby and Johnny stayed together. But Johnny hadn't come back to be with her. He'd come back to make things right for her with her father, and to make things right between them before they said goodbye. Because all that could ever be between those two people who lived in different worlds was that summer fling.

CHAPTER 15

*A*S THE ENGINE ROLLED back up to the firehouse, Hudson leapt down, feeling amped up and ready to take on the world. His adrenaline was high in the wake of the second-story house fire. Three at home. No injuries. The structure itself wasn't a total loss. And he'd had no flashbacks. Not even a tremor. All in all, a good end to his first day back in the field.

Hudson accepted the handshakes and back slaps of the other members of his company.

Carlos Ortega grinned. "It's good to have you back, man."

"Good to be back, Cheech."

"You ready to do some real work after two weeks of lazing around?" This came from Luke Hanover, aka Crash. He hauled out the hose, ready to spray down the engine.

"You remember *how* to do real work after all that?" Aaron Egerton taunted.

"Enough to recognize your lazy ass was on bathroom rotation, Sparky. Your mama'd be ashamed to think that's how you scrub a toilet."

"Sorry to disappoint you, Ma." He blew Hudson a kiss. "I'll get right on that."

Hudson shot up his middle finger and made the rookie laugh.

All around him, his fellow firefighters leapt into action, going through the usual post-fire routines of washing and refilling the truck, divvying up the paperwork, cleaning the turnout gear. As soon as the gear was dealt with, he hit the showers, rinsing off the acrid scent of smoke and sweat. It felt good to be back in the rhythm of the station, part of the crew. It felt good to be useful again.

"Chicken Little's making chili," Ortega announced as they dressed. "You should stick around for that. See the guys on B shift."

"I'll do that." Hudson pulled his phone from his locker and checked his messages.

Audrey: **How did the first day back go?**

And just like that, the yawning void he'd been trying to ignore became center focus again.

Missing her was different from missing John and Steve. They'd been an integral part of the fabric of his days for years. Being back here, even surrounded by the rest of his company, he felt a bit like he was operating without one of his arms. But he was learning to adapt, learning to depend on the others, even if they hadn't developed a life-long mind-meld. Trust was a necessary part of the job. But missing Audrey was a physical ache. Because she was still out there in the world. She just wasn't with him. How had she become such a part of him in only two weeks?

They'd had one last night together after the dance. Charlie had graciously made himself scarce, bunking elsewhere. They'd made the most of it. And instead of making love to her like it was the start of the rest of forever, he'd loved her like it was goodbye. Because it was. She'd tried to convince him it didn't have to be that way. They'd swapped contact information and promises to keep in touch. But each text, each call just ripped the scab off a wound that wasn't healing.

He wanted to hear her voice. To tell her about the day. Instead, he shoved the phone in his pocket without responding and headed for the kitchen. Jason Bradley stood at the stove, stirring a massive pot of chili. From the scents that were wafting his way, Hudson was guessing he'd gone for his four-pepper chili. He hoped like hell there was plenty of sour cream to tone down the heat. A few other guys stood around the table, noshing on tortilla chips and cheese dip.

Jason turned with a wide smile. "Good to see you back, Ma."

Hudson exchanged a back-thumping hug with the other man. "You cubs been behaving?"

"As much as ever. Have you met Hank O'Malley?"

"I haven't."

"Hank, this is Hudson Lowell, aka Ma. Hud, Hank. We call him Pogo. He's a transfer from Boston."

Hudson shook the other man's hand, appreciating that no one verbalized the awkward fact that he was here to replace John. "Decide you're tired of the big ass city?"

"Just wanted a change. The wife wanted to raise our kids in a smaller city."

The stab of envy was swift and unexpected. "How many you got?"

Pogo laughed. "None yet. But we're planning on three and enjoying the hell out of the practice."

As the joking took on a decidedly ribald air, Hudson's mind wandered. Transfer. For the first time since he'd watched Audrey ride away on that bus, he felt a flicker of hope. Maybe he could do with a change. He could fight fires anywhere. His primary reasons for staying here were gone. Maybe he could look into going to California. Would Audrey go for that? Surely, she would. She'd been the one who'd pushed to keep finding a way. Maybe this was it.

His fingers curled around the phone in his pocket just as it began to ring. Heart jolting, he checked the read out. Not Audrey.

"What's up, Rach?"

"Are you done with your shift?" There was a faintly panicked tone to her voice.

"Yeah. What's wrong?"

"My kitchen is flooded. I think the water supply to the dish-washer exploded."

"Did you turn off the main water line?"

She gave an alarmingly watery groan.

Dear God, please don't cry.

"No. John never showed me how. Where is it?"

Hudson gave a wave to the guys and headed for the door as he talked her through the process.

"Okay. I'm sorry to bother you with this, especially coming off a shift, but I could use a hand. And maybe a shop vac."

He felt his hope wink out as fast as it had lit. How could he possibly think of leaving when Rachel was still here? With John gone, there was no one else to take care of her. He owed it to his friend to be there, to help her with whatever she needed. She had to come first.

"I'm on my way."

"I'M HERE to see Dr. Feinstein." Audrey offered the receptionist a smile. "I'm—"

The woman gave a curt nod that had the shellacked ash blonde curls of her short hair bobbing. "Dr. Graham. Of course I remember you from your interview. Welcome back. He's tied up with someone just now. If you'll have a seat."

Audrey lowered herself into one of the low-backed waiting room chairs, rubbing absently at the ache in her legs. It had been a long flight from Tennessee. Whatever happened with this meet-ing, she needed a walk before she went back to the hotel. Pulling out the iPad she'd loaded with research literature, she tried to focus enough to read, but every discussion of survivor's guilt and PTSD had her thinking of Hudson.

Missing him was an ache that rivaled her legs. She hadn't heard from him. Not after the first few days. He'd said it was just too hard and asked for some distance. That had felt like a slap, but what else could she do? He deserved the right to move on. But it hadn't stopped her from thinking about him. She knew he'd gone back to work and was officially slated to be in the field again, taking fire calls. That was his version of getting back to real life. How was he handling it? She had to believe he was being safe, that he wouldn't be allowed back on duty if he was taking reckless risks. But she couldn't help thinking he needed more time to cope with everything that had happened.

"Dr. Graham!"

Audrey looked up as the department head crossed over to her, a broad smile creasing his bearded face. She carefully rose, holding in a wince as her knees protested the motion. "Dr. Feinstein, thank you for meeting with me." Audrey shook the older man's hand.

"Come on back."

She followed him into his office.

He took a seat behind a wide wooden desk, with an old-fashioned leather blotter, and steepled his hands. It was the gesture of a man who knew he was in charge of everything in his domain. "I do hope this visit means you've made your decision to join our faculty."

She'd run the numbers, weighed the pros and cons, and knew that this was the opportunity of a lifetime. But the decision wasn't as cut-and-dried as it might be for anyone else. She wasn't the same woman who'd interviewed here only a few weeks ago.

"May I be frank with you?"

An expression of surprise and perhaps a little concern flitted over his face. "Of course."

"When I interviewed, I explained that I left my position at

Duke because I'd been in an accident, and during my protracted recovery, I could no longer perform my duties as expected."

"Yes. The committee discussed that. It's not a problem for us."

Audrey smiled a little. "I didn't think it was, or you wouldn't have offered me the job." She folded her hands. "I'd like to give you a little more detail."

"I assure you, it has no bearing on your hireability. If you need additional accommodations in the classroom or lab, we can make that happen."

"I appreciate that. But that's not why I want to tell you. My circumstances have direct bearing on my research interests, which I intend to shift from those discussed in my interview."

Feinstein looked intrigued. "Go on."

So, she told him, in broad strokes, about the accident and her subsequent recovery. She'd intended to stop there, sticking to the logical, organized presentation she'd prepared on the flight. Keeping things as professional and clinically distant as possible. But her reasons for pursuing this *were* personal. Deeply so.

"When I left here a few weeks ago, I went to summer camp in the Berkshires."

"Summer camp?" He was clearly wondering where this was going.

Audrey waved that off. "Bucket list. Not the point. While I was there, I met the firefighter who rescued me."

When she'd finished, Feinstein sat back in his big leather chair. He was back to steepling his fingers. "That's…quite the story, Dr. Graham. And I can understand why you'd be moved to do further research in that area. However, that's not a good fit for our department. Perhaps, in a few years, once you've re-established yourself, you can look at branching off—provided you acquire grant funding, of course."

Audrey didn't want to wait years. She didn't want to go back to her old, heartless research. "I appreciate your honesty. But the fact is, this is what I want now. If my accident taught me nothing else, it's that there is no guarantee of tomorrow. I need to do this. I need to shift my research to something that stands to directly impact people in a positive way. I need to make a difference, and I can't do that unless I make a move to applied sociology. I'm not willing to go back to the hours and insanity of tenure track academia unless it's for something I'm passionate about. Life's too short. So, this is what I'm going to pursue." Somewhere. "I understand if you wish to withdraw the offer.

He had a good poker face—no one made department head in academia without it—but she could tell she'd shocked him. What rising academic in their right mind would turn down what they were offering her?

Dr. Feinstein was quiet for a long time, clearly weighing his words. "If that's how you really feel, Dr. Graham, I'm afraid we don't have a place for you at this time."

She'd expected this. But the confirmation still knocked her back and made her grateful for the support of her chair. Some part of her was screaming, *Are you crazy? You can't walk away from this opportunity!* Audrey ignored it, leaning over to grab her purse from the floor. "I completely understand. And I apologize for wasting your and the committee's time." She started to rise.

"Wait. You also have a Masters in clinical psychology, do you not?"

It was the last thing she'd expected him to ask. "I haven't used it for anything, and I'm not licensed to practice, but yes."

"I have a colleague who'd be very interested in speaking with you. Rhona Prescott over at Syracuse."

Audrey's breath caught. "But their department isn't hiring." She'd checked that from the airport as she and Sam waited on their flight back to Tennessee.

"She's not in the sociology department. She's a research professor—part of a joint program with the VA hospital there. I think she'd really appreciate your story." He picked up the phone. "Let me make a call."

CHAPTER 16

*A*UDREY WAS GREEN BY the time she arrived at the firehouse. That hadn't been the plan, but she'd been more optimistic than she should've been about driving down I-31 for the first time since the accident. Maybe she should've taken a circuitous route through the city instead of the interstate. Too late now. She'd fought off the panic attack, so to her mind, the whole experience had been a win. Except for the fact that she was clammy with anxiety sweat and still feeling nauseous. Only some of that was from the panic attack.

It seemed her chest had been tight from the moment the bus had left Camp Firefly Falls. As if she couldn't quite take a full breath away from Hudson. Stupid. But the sensation hadn't gone away. It had been three weeks since she'd had any contact with him. Three weeks during which she'd moved heaven and earth. Three weeks in which she'd changed her whole life.

It would be worth it. It had to be.

She climbed out of her car and smoothed her hands over the skirt that was already smooth, then strode toward the four-bay fire station. One of the bay doors was up, and she cautiously stepped inside. 'Hello?"

A head popped out from behind the big truck in front of her. "Help you ma'am?"

"I'm looking for Hudson Lowell."

The young man, who couldn't have been more than twenty, came toward her, wiping his hands on a towel. "He's not here."

"Oh." Flummoxed, Audrey just stood there. She'd been so busy rehearsing what she wanted to say, she hadn't given any thought to the fact that he might've changed shifts or taken a day off. Or what if going back out on calls hadn't worked? What if he'd had a relapse of his PTSD symptoms?

Another man stepped out of a room off to the side. "What's going on?"

The young guy jerked a thumb in her direction. "She's looking for Ma."

Ma? "Beg your pardon?" Audrey asked.

"Hudson."

"You call him Ma?"

The second man strode over and flashed a grin. "Nickname. Because he's always taking care of everybody, like a den mother."

"Yeah, he's good about that," she said, and ached. "I'll just call him. Thanks." She'd wanted to surprise him.

That's not why you didn't call in the first place.

She'd been afraid he wouldn't answer, or, worse, he'd tell her he didn't want to see her.

As Audrey turned to leave, a woman dressed in cargo pants and an SFD t-shirt materialized from somewhere. She gave Audrey the once over. "He's up at the picnic."

"Picnic?"

"Yeah, the department's sponsoring a big picnic for the Fourth. He was on first shift here this morning so he could attend this afternoon."

Suddenly Audrey felt stupid. It was the Fourth of July. She'd been so focused on everything else, she hadn't considered the holiday. He'd be with family and friends, probably. Busy. Surrounded by people. Her belly clutched again.

He's going to want to see you. You're not coming all this way and chickening out.

She squared her shoulders. "Where?"

They gave her directions. Twenty minutes later, she finally found parking and began the hike through the park, looking for a familiar set of broad shoulders. Scents of grilling meat and fried dough permeated the air. As the nausea faded, her stomach began to growl, reminding her it was coming up on dinner. But she didn't want to meet Hudson again with a hot dog or funnel cake in her hands.

There were people everywhere. Families. Children. Clusters of friends. Lines snaked out from vendor tents and assorted games. How would she ever find him amid this crowd? She set up a mental grid and began to crisscross the park, methodically scanning faces. Daylight was fading. All around her, people were setting up lawn chairs and blankets, talking about the fireworks to come. She was running out of time. Maybe she should just give up until tomorrow. Call him like a sane person. Wrestling with disappointment, she turned back toward the parking lot.

And there he was. Smiling. With a tall, willowy blonde in his arms.

Audrey stopped dead, her stomach dropping to her toes, her chest cranking like a vise. After everything they'd shared, everything he'd said, she hadn't expected he could move on so fast. But they had no understanding. They'd had no future. There was nothing stopping him from finding a rebound, moving on to someone else.

Pulling back from his embrace, the blonde saw her first. Her brows shot up, and she said something to Hudson. He turned, surprise flickering over his face. Audrey couldn't make herself move, not to approach him and not to retreat. Her heart beat an erratic tattoo against her ribs and her palms went damp.

Hudson said something to his companions—because of course he was with a group. His family, probably. And everybody was staring at her. He made it over to her in less than a dozen strides. There was no quick, impulsive hug, no kiss hello. He looked... guarded and wary.

"Hi," she managed, hating the catch in her voice.

"Hi, yourself."

Audrey knew she was staring and couldn't seem to stop. She drank in the sight of him, absorbing the snug fit of his gray t-shirt across his broad, capable shoulders, and the faint shadow of stubble on his solid jaw. Her tongue felt thick and clumsy, and the carefully prepared speech she'd been rehearsing simply disappeared. "God, it's good to see you."

She wanted to throw herself into his arms, but he didn't look happy to see her. He didn't look angry either. Audrey didn't know what to do with this neutrality. She couldn't read him, and that made her anxiety crank higher. Maybe this was a mistake.

Hudson jerked his head. "Come and meet my family."

The nerves ratcheted up another notch as he led her over to the group, who looked on with undisguised curiosity.

"Everybody, this is Audrey Graham."

Half a dozen people nodded or waved at her.

Hudson reeled off introductions, most of which Audrey was too rattled to catch. He gestured to the blonde he'd been hugging. "And this is Rachel."

John's widow. Audrey glanced at Hudson and got a tiny confirmatory nod. So maybe that hadn't been what she'd thought. Still, none of this was going how she'd planned.

Use your manners. "Pleased to meet you all."

"I'm thrilled to meet you." Rachel stepped in, giving Audrey a hard hug.

Startled, Audrey could only stand there, wooden, as the other woman squeezed.

"Thank you for giving him back to us," she whispered.

Nothing in her repository of proper social behavior seemed the right response to that, so she gave Rachel an awkward half-hug in return. "You're welcome?"

"Hudson's told me so much about you," Rachel continued, stepping back as if they hadn't just shared one of the world's most awkward hugs.

Uncertain, Audrey glanced at Hudson, but he was still doing an impression of a stone wall.

Hudson's mom, Janie, smiled. "How do you know Hudson, dear?"

"That's...a little complicated. Your son saved my life two years ago."

Predictably, several pairs of eyes flicked downward to the legs left exposed by her summer sundress. Hudson briefly pressed a hand to the small of her back. The automatic gesture of support and reassurance loosened some of the knots in her stomach.

"We reconnected at camp," she finished, feeling lame and awkward and wishing they could go somewhere private to talk.

Before she could ask him, the younger woman—Hudson's sister?—asked, "What brings you to Syracuse?"

Audrey didn't want to get into this with a crowd. She had so much she needed to say to him, to explain. But they were all looking at her, waiting for some kind of answer. "Business." The word tripped from her tongue automatically and felt wrong. It hadn't been business that had brought her to Syracuse.

"Oh yeah? What do you do?" Janie asked.

"She's a research professor at Berkeley," Hudson replied. There was a curious mix of pride and strain in his tone.

Audrey met his eyes. "No, I'm not." She wanted to get that out there as fast as possible, since telling him about Berkeley in the first place had been the moment she'd felt what was between them fracture.

It was only as Hudson went utterly still that she realized he'd been practically vibrating with nervous energy. "What do you mean you're not?"

"I went to California. Once I told them about the change in my direction of research, they didn't want me."

A crease appeared between his brows. Audrey wanted to kiss it smooth. "I don't understand. They already offered you the job."

"They offered me a job based on a continuation of the research I began at Duke. They weren't interested in applied sociology, and at this point, I'm not willing to do anything else." This was more than she'd meant to say in front of their audience, but she had Hudson's undivided attention now and knew she couldn't leave him hanging.

"I've been in mainstream academia my entire career. Hell, my entire life. After the accident, all I could think about was getting back on track. Then I met you. And you made me want—" *You.* "— something different. Something more. So, I left California, and I came here."

"Here?" The word was sharp, and she could see the lines of tension beneath his carefully blank expression.

"The thing about academia is that it's a terribly small world. The department chair at Berkeley put me in touch with a former colleague of his—Rhoda Prescott. She holds a joint appointment between Syracuse University and the VA hospital. She's starting a new program working with veterans on coping with PTSD and reintegration into society. I convinced her to hire me to develop a new branch of the program on coping with survivor's guilt."

A muscle jumped in Hudson's jaw.

Audrey felt a flutter of panic. What if he didn't understand? What if he thought her shift in research was because she thought he was damaged? That she thought she could fix him?

She knotted her hands. "I meant what I told you before, that I couldn't imagine going back to the rigors of academia unless it was for something that really mattered. I want to help people. You just helped me figure out the focus."

Hudson was staring at her. "So, you walked away from a shot at Berkeley, changed your entire research focus, practically produced a job out of thin air, and turned your entire life on its ear—because of me?"

Her knees felt loose and her stomach dipped like she was at the top of a precipice. "Do you remember what you said to me that day at the top of the ropes course?"

"You'll have to take the leap."

Audrey nodded once and spread her hands, feeling exposed and vulnerable and more terrified than she'd been in her entire life. "I'm taking it. No guidewire, no safety harness, no net." *Oh please, catch me.*

Tension radiated off him in waves, but still, he said nothing.

She swallowed. "If you've changed your mind, I understand. We haven't even talked in—"

She didn't finish the thought, didn't finish the breath, because suddenly his hands were buried in her hair and his mouth was a fever on hers. All the days and all the miles of distance evaporated. Heart leaping, she fisted her hands in his shirt and kissed him back—at least until the applause and whistles started. Blood rushing to her cheeks, she broke away, feeling twin urges to laugh and cry with relief.

"Twenty-six days," he breathed.

Audrey blinked at him. "What?"

"Since we last talked. Twenty-six days, nine hours, and somewhere around forty minutes, give or take. I'm not sure what time you got here. Time kinda stopped." His eyes warmed with a smile, like the sun sparking off the surface of the ocean. "I've been counting."

The clamp around her chest loosened, and she took her first full breath in a month. Relief had her sagging against him.

Hudson tightened his hold, taking her weight. "You okay?"

"So okay. It's just, you've melted my knees again." She aimed for a stern expression and missed by a mile, unable to repress a grin. "Terrible habit of yours."

His smile was blinding. "Who needs knees anyway? You've got me."

And that, Audrey thought, as he kissed her again, hard and fast, was everything she'd ever needed.

EPILOGUE

*T*HE CAMP FIREFLY FALLS bus was pulling out of the gravel lot as Hudson turned into it. People were milling everywhere, cheerfully greeting old friends and bouncing between the stack of luggage that had been offloaded and the registration table.

Rachel took one look at the chaos and said, "Maybe this was a bad idea."

What a difference a year makes, Hudson mused as he climbed out of the Jeep. "It's a great idea. You need some time away, just like I did."

His cousin turned fretful eyes toward Audrey. "But I hate to leave you with the group all by yourself."

Audrey smiled and took Rachel by the arms. "The group will be *fine*. All the new guys are doing great. They're taking to the baking like ducks to water."

Who knew that a bunch of taciturn, struggling, ex-military men would find new purpose as bakers, of all things? Well, Audrey had. She'd co-opted Rachel's commercial baking expertise and pioneered a new reintegration program involving a combination of skills training and therapy. The pilot study had shown great promise—enough that Audrey had landed a five-year grant to evaluate the program more in depth.

"But—" Rachel began.

"No buts. I've got this," Audrey told her firmly. "You've been pulling the workaholic routine for a year. It's time for a break and Camp Firefly Falls is the perfect opportunity. You're going to love it."

To settle the issue, Hudson hauled Rachel's massive duffel to the registration table, where Heather Tully sat with her clipboard and a mile-wide smile.

"Hudson! I didn't know you were joining us again this summer."

"I'm not. My cousin is. Rachel McCleary. We're dropping her off."

"We?" Heather asked.

Audrey ducked under his arm and snuggled close. "We."

"Audrey! How good to see you. I'd ask how you're doing, but it's obvious you're happy. You're glowing."

"They're disgustingly happy," Rachel put in with a smile. "It's adorable."

It had taken Hudson a while to get accustomed to her enthusiastic support of his relationship with Audrey. He'd worried that being openly in love around her would make John's absence that much more apparent. But while she'd grieved hard and long, she'd made it abundantly clear that seeing him happy was helping her heal. It hadn't hurt that she and Audrey had become fast friends.

Hudson made introductions. "I trust you'll take good care of her while she's here."

"Of course, we will." Heather handed over the welcome packet and began giving the spiel. "One of our staff will take you to your cabin." She waved and a familiar blond guy trotted over.

"Charlie!" Audrey broke away to give Charlie a big hug.

Charlie grinned as he hugged her back. "Well, I'll be damned. Y'all worked it out."

"We did, indeed."

Hudson chuckled to himself. *Greet old friends at camp.* She was getting to cross something else off her list. There weren't too many things left. It had been one of his greatest pleasures to make sure of that as she'd settled into her new life in Syracuse. Sometime around Christmas he'd started his own list of things he wanted to see and do with her. He was hoping he'd be crossing the first one off today.

"What are you doing as staff?" he asked.

"I have left the book business." Charlie said it in a tone that clearly implied, *It's complicated.* "Since I was at loose ends for the summer, I thought being a counselor here was a good chance to re-evaluate my life and figure out what's next."

"Seems like that's going around," Rachel muttered.

"Camp is good for that," Audrey declared.

And thank God for it. He didn't really want to think where he'd be if Audrey hadn't come back into his life.

"I wish you two were going to be here with me," Rachel pouted.

Audrey squeezed her tight. "I know. Me, too. We'll schedule far enough out for next summer that we can all get time off. Meanwhile, you have a *great* time! Don't do anything I wouldn't do."

"You did everything while you were here," Hudson reminded her.

Audrey grinned. "Exactly."

Hudson hugged Rachel himself, hoping Camp Firefly Falls was as good an experience for her as it had been for him. "Have fun. We'll see you in two weeks."

Charlie hefted Rachel's bag and made a sweeping gesture toward the trail. "After you, madam."

They said their goodbyes. Audrey looked at the trails leading up to camp proper, her expression full of nostalgia. "I really do wish we'd been able to come this summer."

Hudson laced his hands behind her back. "Want to take a walk around the lake before we get back on the road? Stretch your legs?"

"Oh, that sounds good. And maybe we can stop at Boone's for a slice of pie on the way home?" She turned those big, baby blues on him, and he was a goner.

"Anything you want."

They took the trail up to camp, around the lodge, on past the boat house to the pier. It looked exactly the same as last summer, but he felt so totally different. All because of this woman.

Hudson tugged her back against him, pressing a kiss to the top of her head as they looked out over the sparkling water of Lake Waawaatesi. "You know, I was standing right here the first time I saw you last summer."

"When I followed you out from the dance."

"No. I saw you from across the lake. Right over there." He pointed to the trail, where a trio of women walked and talked, their laughter floating on the breeze. "You were taking a walk, probably stretching your legs like today, and I envied you."

"Why?"

"You looked so contented and peaceful. And I was so...not." He turned her to face him. "But you gave me that. You pulled me out of myself and taught me that living isn't just the best way to honor my friends, it's the brave choice. You always make the brave choice. And that makes you *my* hero."

Her eyes were already glimmering with emotion. "Hudson. All I did was love you."

"It's the best thing that's ever happened to me. You're the best thing that's ever happened to me. The past year with you has been the best of my life. That's why I brought you back up here today. It felt like it had to be here."

"What does?"

"The beginning of everything." Hudson took a step back, dropping to one knee and pulling the ring box from his cargo shorts. "I love you, Audrey. I want to make a life, a family with you. To grow old with you. Say you'll marry me. Be my wife, my everything."

Audrey pressed a hand to her mouth. The tears spilled over and Hudson's stomach bottomed out. Maybe it was too soon. Maybe doing it here was a mistake. Maybe—

"Yes." She dropped her hands and reached for him, her smile beaming like the sun. "Yes, I'll marry you."

Relief burst through him, and he surged to his feet, scooping her off hers with a celebratory whoop. Applause and cheers broke out from somewhere behind them. Hudson stopped spinning to see that several dozen people lined the bank. Charlie and Rachel were at the head of the pack.

Charlie cupped a hand around his mouth. "Kiss!"

Rachel picked up the cry, until the entire pack was chanting it.

Audrey laughed and lifted her face to his. "Better give the people what they want."

"You already gave me what I wanted," he said, and closed the distance.

Choose Your Next Romance

For more camp shenanigans, keep turning the pages to read *Once Upon A Campfire*, a Meet Cute Romance set earlier that summer. It's a twin-impersonation story that will tickle the fancy of anybody who loved *The Parent Trap!*

Audrey's BFF Sam is from a little town called Eden's Ridge, Tennessee. Sam's story is a twofer that's part of the Men of the Misfit Inn series. It begins with *Until We Meet Again* (a prequel novella) and continues in *Come a Little Closer* (Book 4) but you can visit her hometown, starting with *When You Got a Good Thing*, the first book in The Misfit Inn quartet that introduces the Eden's Ridge Universe.

Keep turning pages to get a sneak peek!

ONCE UPON A CAMPFIRE

A CAMP FIREFLY FALLS MEET CUTE ROMANCE BONUS STORY

It was a terrible idea.

But that doesn't stop Sarah Meadows from saying yes to covering for her identical twin sister at staff orientation week at Camp Firefly Falls. It's just a few days and she'll be back to finishing her master's thesis, right? But when her sexy, ex-park ranger partner figures out her secret, she's got her work cut out convincing him not to turn her in.

Beckett Hayes knows he should report Sarah to the boss, but instead, he finds himself agreeing to train her. There's just something about those big, doe eyes and all that sass. But when Sarah starts to matter more than he planned, the pressure's on. Can he convince her to take the road less traveled or will this one week have to be enough?

"I NEED YOU TO impersonate me."

From the faded corduroy sofa in her tiny, studio apartment, Sarah Meadows rolled her eyes, though her sister on the other end of the phone couldn't see. "Did you forget to renew your driver's license again? Because it expired back in January."

"I wish it were something that simple," Taylor said. "I've got a serious problem."

"What is it this time?" Sarah tried to keep the judgment out of her voice. Really, she did. But it was hard. So much of her twin's adult life had been a train wreck, and it seemed Sarah was routinely the one called upon to pick up the pieces.

"Well, you know I was supposed to be done with this private tour guide gig day after tomorrow and flying back East in time to start the new job at Camp Firefly Falls on Saturday, right?"

"Yeah. You've got orientation next week."

"I'm not going to make it back in time."

Oh, not good. Not good at all. "Did your flight get canceled?"

"No. This job came in last night—a week-long trek for some Hollywood muckitymuck."

"You are *not* blowing off the camp job for one last guide trip." Dear God, she'd thought Taylor was past this kind of thing.

"No, it's not like that. I told Danny I couldn't do it. But he's threatening not to give me my last month's pay if I don't stick around and do it."

"You haven't been paid in a *month?*"

"Room and board were covered, and I figured if I didn't have the money in hand, I couldn't blow it on anything stupid. Except now I risk not getting paid at all, and I need that money, Sarah."

That was putting things mildly. Three years before, Taylor's unfortunate taste in men had resulted in a short relationship with one Jax Howorth—not his real name—who'd taken every dime of Taylor's money, trashed her credit, and left her in a mountain of debt. She'd been slowly, painstakingly climbing out of that hole ever since.

Sarah sighed. "How much are we talking?"

Her sister named a figure that had Sarah's mouth dropping open.

"You're getting paid that much as a guide?" Maybe she'd chosen the wrong career. Not that anybody became a grad student to make money. The hope was that you'd make some when you finished the degree.

"Rich people will pay for all kinds of things. And this producer guy, or whoever, is willing to give me a five *thousand* dollar bonus to stick around."

That had all of Sarah's alarm bells ringing. "Are you sure he doesn't expect you to do something more than be a trail guide?"

"Positive. He's flamingly gay."

Well, that was something, at least. "So, what exactly are you asking?"

"I want you to go to Camp Firefly Falls and be me for orientation week. I'll be done with this job, get paid, and be back in time for the certification test. Nobody will be any the wiser."

Exasperated, Sarah shoved to her feet and began to pace. Ten steps to the kitchen. Fifteen to the window overlooking the busy Brooklyn street. Five to her bedroom door, then start again. "Taylor, this isn't like fooling our high school teachers. This is a job! One that you're qualified for and I'm not. And what about you actually learning the stuff you're being certified *for?*"

"I've learned the handbook backwards and forwards, and there's nothing a camp in the Berkshires can throw at me that's harder than what I've been doing in Wyoming."

"That may be, but *I'm* not trained for any of this! How do you expect anybody to believe that I'm you?"

"It's not that complicated, sis. You're in good shape. You're a trained lifeguard, a runner. And God knows, you haven't met a subject you can't study up on and pass a test for. You just have to spend a week learning their policies and procedures, helping get camp set up, readying cabins, and that kind of thing. Easy peasy."

"Yeah, that's what you said when you convinced me to fill in at cheerleading practice so you could meet up with that college guy. 'Kick high, shake your thing, you'll be fine,' you said, 'they'll never know the difference.' Only you failed to mention the pyramid, and trust me, when it all came down, everyone knew the difference."

There was a noise at the other end of the line that sounded suspiciously like a stifled snort of laughter. Taylor cleared her throat. "In my defense, I didn't think they would try the pyramid. Man they were pissed."

"Not making your case here, Tay."

"But pissed at me, they were pissed at me. And no human pyramid at camp, no polyester, and no shaking your thing unless you're so inclined. But preferably not, because, you know, I have to work with these people."

"I'm smarter than I was at seventeen. Too smart to let you drag me into this. Besides, I do have a life. Responsibilities. I can't just pick up and go play you for a week."

"Oh, come on. Like you can't take a week off from your thesis?"

"I can't, actually. I'm on a very strict schedule in order to finish in time to defend in August and start the doctoral program in the fall." She'd scrimped and saved in order to take the summer off from any assistantships so she could just write and be done with the thing. She wasn't about to waste that time.

"But just imagine how much clearer your head will be after getting out of the city. You said yourself, you have a hard time writing there. You've been dying to get out of New York. This is your chance to recharge a little. And it's beautiful. You could take your camera, finally have some of the nature you actually *like* shooting pictures of."

A car horn blared from the street below and somebody shouted an inventive curse in...was that Portuguese?

A muscle by Sarah's eye began to twitch. "By working for you."

"Pleeeeeeease," Taylor wheedled. "Think about it, Sarah! Five *thousand*. It's enough to put a serious dent in the stupid debt. Enough I might be able to pay the last of it off by the end of the summer, so I can finally have a clean slate."

A clean slate. That had been Taylor's Holy Grail since Jax walked out of her life. He'd been her wakeup call, the last in a long line of poor decisions. The school of hard knocks had taught her what no one else could, and she was finally ready to grow up. If she finally could get free of the mess Jax had created, she'd be able to do that. And Sarah would be able to stop worrying about her and focus on her own work. Maybe.

But could she really afford a week away?

The living room wall rattled as something solid slammed against it from the apartment next door. A moan and the rhythmic thumping that followed told her it was the newlyweds going at it again, instead of a nice, helpful home invasion that would put an end to the ear-splitting noise violations they engaged in multiple times a day. The eye-twitch ramped up to a full on headache. Not only were they supremely distracting, their enthusiastic amour only served to highlight exactly how long it had been since there'd been a man in her life.

Not that she was looking.

Sarah pinched the bridge of her nose. "You *swear* this is something I can pull off?"

"Absolutely!" Taylor assured her.

She was probably going to regret this. But maybe her twin was right and getting back to nature would help break the writer's block that had been plaguing her for months. At the very least, maybe she'd get some shots to replace the artwork on her walls.

"Okay, I'm in. Tell me what I need to do."

"Good morning, staffers!"

From one of the picnic tables set up down by Lake Waawaatesi, Beckett Hayes watched his new boss, Heather Tully, address the assembled crowd. Oh yeah. His buddy, Michael, had done well when he'd married her. The cheerful blonde looked absolutely in her element. And why shouldn't she? Camp Firefly Falls—summer camp for grown-ups—was her brain child.

"It's going to be a super busy week as we finish prepping for our first session of the summer—Singles Week—so we'll be throwing you all into the deep end with that one."

"Deep end is right," the guy next to him whispered. "I was here for that last year. It's like policing a damned orgy."

"Lovely," Beckett muttered. He'd dealt with some of that in his last job as national park ranger. Herding drunk, horny people was never fun. It almost always ended in insults and often with beer or other questionable liquids spilled on his uniform.

"Now, some of you will be here all summer and some will be in and out, depending on the specifics of the session, but everybody has to pass their camp certification by the end of the week to keep our insurance company happy. That said, we want all of you to have fun yourselves. Here at Camp Firefly Falls, we work hard and play hard. The work begins bright and early at eight every morning. You can pick up your daily assignments at breakfast. We wrap in time for dinner at six, with evening activities planned so you can get to know your fellow staff members."

The collective staff cheered.

"This afternoon, we're getting started with a swim test."

"Are you serious?" someone called from down front.

"Camp rules. Everybody has to tread water for two minutes, then swim out to the raft and back. Anybody who does not pass will *not* be on any water activities for the summer. Anybody who's not already suited up, go change. We get rolling in fifteen minutes!"

Beckett held himself back from the minor stampede toward the staff cabins to change clothes. He was already set with board shorts and a t-shirt. While waiting, he scanned the remaining faces, noting the animated conversations and laughter. A lot of these people were returning staff, and a fair chunk had been campers here before the Tullys bought it and turned it into a resort, back when Camp Firefly Falls had been a regular sleep-away camp for kids.

Beckett hadn't been one of them.

Michael wandered over and plunked down on the other side of the table. "Settling in okay?"

"Getting there."

"Cabin working out for you?"

Beckett laughed. "It's like a damned penthouse suite compared to some of the places I lived with the park service. Listen, I want to thank you again for giving me a job this summer. After the—" He cut himself off, not wanting to get into the mess of his former position. "Well, my prospects weren't great. This is really saving my ass." The summer's work would buy him time to figure out his next move.

"Hey, it's our gain and my pleasure. They were wrong for firing you."

Beckett jerked his shoulders. "Yeah, well, I was far from the only one. You flagrantly disagree with the powers that be, you get burned." Even given how things had turned out, he couldn't regret being part of the AltPark movement. It was good work. Important work. Work that was now being carried out by others.

They both looked out over the lake, glistening in the early morning sun. It was gorgeous, soothing, and a far cry from the Ivy League campus where they'd met.

"Never would have thought we'd end up here when we were busting our humps for our MBAs," Beckett observed.

"Maybe not me, but you walked away from the crazy a lot sooner than I did."

In his last year of grad school, Beckett had walked out. Of the classroom. Of the MBA program. Away from Dartmouth. He'd never looked back. "Wasn't gonna make me happy."

"I wish I'd figured the same out sooner. That whole corporate culture nearly cost me my wife."

"But it didn't," Beckett observed. "This place brought you two back together."

Michael sighed in obvious contentment. "Seems fitting since we were camp sweethearts as kids."

He tipped back his water. "You're a lucky bastard."

"Yes, yes I am. And hey, who knows? Maybe you'll meet your match this summer."

Beckett cocked an eyebrow at his friend. "Come on, now. I expect that kind of crap from Heather. Not from you."

Michael just grinned. "We've got a bulletin board up in Pinecone Lodge with pictures of all the couples who've gotten together here. It's filling up."

"You, sir, are full of shit."

Laughing, Michael shoved back from the table. "Just don't let Heather hear you say that. She'll try to matchmake you."

"I do not need the complication of a woman in my life."

"They're the only complication that's worth it." Spoken like the happily married man he was.

"And on that saccharine note, I believe I'll take my position at the starting line." Beckett stripped off his t-shirt and toed off his Chacos, leaving them in a neat pile on the picnic table as he went to join the thickening crowd on the dock.

He found himself next to a long, lean woman bent in a forward fold. He made a valiant effort not to stare at her ass in the snug, racer-back swimsuit and ended up admiring her gorgeously toned legs instead.

"See something you like?" The wry tone had him yanking his eyes away like a teenage boy caught peeping in the girls' locker room.

Busted.

"Sorry," Beckett muttered, gaze now firmly on the raft anchored out in Lake Waawaatesi. "You just look—" Was there any way to finish that sentence that didn't make him come off like a perv? "—like you know what you're doing."

"I should. I've been swimming competitively practically since birth." She straightened. "I'm Taylor."

He interpreted the proffered hand as a sign of forgiveness and turned to take it. His own name died on his tongue as he found himself faced with the biggest doe eyes he'd ever seen.

Well hello, Bambi.

"Hi."

A corner of Taylor's mouth quirked as she gave his hand a perfunctory shake. "May the best swimmer win."

"Win wha—"

The scream of an air horn signaled the start of the test. Taylor dove for the water, as did everyone around Beckett before he could get his brain in gear. She'd already surfaced by the time he dove in. The chill lake water was a shock to his system, clearing the haze of lust from his brain.

"Two minutes!" shouted Heather. "Starting…now!"

His feet and arms automatically began to tread, keeping him afloat. A few feet away, Taylor was already facing the raft, her dark hair slicked back like a seal.

"In a hurry?" he asked.

She glanced over her shoulder. "Eye on the target."

"You know this isn't a contest, right?"

Her lips bowed into a full-on grin that sucker punched him more than the icy lake. "Everything's a competition."

Beckett had done everything in his power to get away from competition in his life. But something about that smile pulled at him and invited him to join in the fun. He had a feeling competition with Taylor would be anything but the senseless, boring grind he'd walked away from. So he readied muscles honed as a boy in the surf off Myrtle Beach, and when Heather blew the air horn again, he went for it.

He made it to the head of the pack in four strokes, but Taylor was faster. Her freestyle was a thing of beauty, slicing cleanly through the water as if she'd been born to it. Beckett dug deep, pulling his focus back to his own form. Half a dozen strokes and he'd closed the gap to two lengths. Ahead, Taylor slapped the raft and dove, popping back up and heading toward shore. Beckett tagged the raft himself and switched to butterfly for the return leg. He caught up with her at the halfway point. Seeing what he was about, she shifted smoothly into a butterfly stroke herself, and they both raced for the finish line.

Taylor beat him by two strokes. Beckett could hear her crow of victory as she slapped the dock.

"You are a freaking mermaid," he gasped.

She slicked her hair back and beamed. "Yes, I am. God, that felt good!"

A shadow fell over the two of them. Michael. "You realize we have no prizes, right?"

"Maybe you should," Beckett suggested. "Because that was damned impressive."

"Maybe we'll just move things around so she's on lifeguard duty instead of paired up with you for rock climbing."

"Looks like tomorrow we get to go to *my* playground." Beckett grinned, turning to the mermaid. Something had wiped the smile clear off her face. In fact, she looked a little sick. What was that about?

The lodge was buzzing with conversation, when Sarah stumbled in at 7:15 the next morning. She didn't make eye contact with anyone, didn't talk. Her entire attention was focused on finding the coffee. As long as she got some in the next two minutes, no one would get maimed, and she'd probably manage to maintain her cover.

"Good morning."

Sarah held in a whimper. How dare anyone expect her to converse before caffeine? Homicide on her mind, she turned to find a mug held out to her.

"Oh, thank Jesus." She snatched it from the big, masculine hand, and took a hefty swallow, not caring that the coffee scalded her mouth. The heat from the mug soaked through her hands, taming the beast and melting away her habitual foul greeting of the day.

Lifting her gaze, she found her competition from the swim test yesterday. He was grinning at her, clearly amused. Sarah didn't even care. He'd brought her coffee. As far as she was concerned, that was a life debt. "You, my friend, have just performed an act of the greatest public service. No one will die today."

"Glad to hear it. Since there was no official prize for winning yesterday, I figured not having to fix your first official cup of camp coffee would have to do."

"Better than any trophy. Come to me, my sweet, sweet nectar of the gods." She took another sip, slower this time, and rolled it around in her mouth, savoring with a contented sigh. It was excellent coffee—rich and bold and black as midnight.

He laughed. "Not a morning person, I take it."

"Not even a little bit."

As the fog of sleep began to lift, Sarah took a moment to study her benefactor. He looked annoyingly bright-eyed, his Camp Firefly Falls t-shirt stretched across the broad shoulders that she now knew could execute a perfect butterfly. That was almost sexier than the sculpted chest she could still picture with rivulets of water running down to the board shorts that hung, dripping, low on his lean hips.

And why are you cataloging his finer features? You won't be here to enjoy them after this week.

Perhaps her man-drought was taking its toll, but there was no harm in admiring the view. He'd done the same to her on the dock. And hadn't that been a nice boost to her ego? After all the time sitting on her ass in classrooms and labs or camped out in study carrels, she still had something worth admiring. She lifted her gaze to his face. Not classically handsome or the vaguely geek-chic she'd become accustomed to in academia, but his was an appealing face. All sharp angles and scruff. He'd be next to the picture of *rugged* in the dictionary. Who knew that worked for her?

Sarah lifted the mug. "And to whom do I owe this beneficence? I didn't catch your name yesterday."

"Beckett Hayes. And you're Taylor the Mermaid."

Sadly, for this week, yes.

Since he'd brought her coffee, she graced him with a smile. "Meadows. Taylor Meadows. Nice to meet you." Taking another sip, Sarah glanced around. "You seem to know the lay of the land. Where are our schedules?"

"Right this way." Beckett led her across the room to a table set up at the tail end of the buffet.

The schedules had been alphabetized by last name. Sarah found hers and skimmed it.

"According to Heather, the staff has been split into four groups for orientation." As Beckett continued to talk, Sarah skimmed the list. "We'll all be rotating through the assorted classes—first aid, CPR—"

"Bartending? Really?"

"So I'm told." He shrugged. "Anyway, between all that, we'll be doing overall prep of the facilities and checking equipment."

That didn't sound so bad. When Michael Tully had mentioned she'd been assigned to rock climbing, she'd nearly panicked. But Taylor was entirely qualified to deal with that, and she'd be here to take her rightful place by the end of the week. Sarah had eyes in her head. Surely she could look at the equipment to check it for frays or weak spots or any other sign that it was worn out. There wouldn't be time to actually climb anything with everything else going on. Taylor had *promised* there'd be no human pyramid equivalent at this orientation.

"Which group are you in?" she asked.

"Red."

"Same as me." That pleased her far more than it should. But what was the harm in enjoying a little flirtation for a few days?

Beckett peered over her shoulder at her afternoon assignments. "And looks like Michael kept you with me for rock climbing, after all. I figure the plan for today will be to meet the other staff on that rotation, do an equipment inventory, and start checking out the available climbs for campers."

Michael had said something similar yesterday, but the implications hadn't sunk in. They did now.

"Are you the head rock climbing guy?" Sarah hoped her voice sounded casual.

"So they tell me. Everything around here is a cakewalk compared to Yosemite, which is where I spent the last three years in the National Park Service. If I make it through the summer without having to use my S and R skills, I'll be thrilled."

He was a freaking park ranger. Who'd apparently done search and rescue in California. Which meant he knew his shit. Great for the camp. Not great for her. He was liable to figure out in less than five minutes that she was green as grass, when it came to rock climbing.

Beckett steered her toward the breakfast buffet. "Better eat up. It's gonna be a long day."

"Greeeeeeat."

How on Earth was she going to keep her cover as Taylor?

∾

Taylor Meadows knew her first aid. She sailed through the class, hand up, voice clear and confident as she readily answered questions. Beckett decided it was true what people said—confidence really was sexy. The legs certainly didn't hurt. And damn, he'd had dreams about those legs last night.

As the session broke up, Michael bumped Beckett's shoulder. "Doesn't look like Heather's services as Cupid are necessary."

"Huh?"

"You've had your eye on the pretty brunette since the swim test yesterday."

Had he been that obvious? "Just enjoying the view."

Michael smirked. "Pinecone Lodge, man. Pinecone Lodge."

Beckett gave him a friendly shove. "Shut up."

His buddy only laughed.

"Yeah yeah, whatever. I've got work to do," Beckett announced.

Over lunch, he made the switch from student to instructor, calling all of his people together at the end of the meal. "The plan for today is inventory of equipment, both ours and the gear meant for the ziplines and ropes course. And a quick tour of the most common climbing locations around camp."

Taylor's hand went up. "Might I suggest we do the tour first? It would be a nice mental break after the morning's classes."

It was six of one, half dozen of the other to him. "Sure. We can do that."

Beckett took them to the trail leading to Base Camp Adventure Park, where the zip lines and ropes course were set up. They walked the length of the various activities, discussed assignments, then he led the pack back to Boulder Mountain.

"This is our primary climb site. As you can see, there are three main paths up, separated out by experience level. Nothing here is above an intermediate skillset, as the majority of campers probably will have little to no experience," he explained.

"What about experienced climbers? Don't we have a Scout Wars session later this summer?" Diego asked.

"We'll take those on a case-by-case basis. Taylor and I will be scouting prospective locations around the camp property, as well as in the adjacent state park later this week." It seemed like the ideal means of spending some one-on-one time with her.

She went brows up. "We will?"

Beckett would've felt better if she'd said it with the same amused snark she'd used when she'd caught him checking out her legs, instead of that faint look of panic. Had he done something to offend her? Maybe he'd read her signals entirely wrong. Maybe she wasn't actually interested or had changed her mind. In which case, fine. He could keep this professional. "Based on everyone's applications, you've got the most climbing experience besides me." He'd verified that himself last night by reviewing the applicants assigned to him.

She just nodded, looking faintly green.

Definitely something going on there. A bad fall? Scared to get back on the mountain? *Later,* he promised himself, when they weren't surrounded by other staff.

Back at the equipment shed, he divided up the group. "I want each of you to count and check your assigned component. Make note of any prospective issues with the gear you see. Diego, you're on harnesses. Break down the count by men's and women's. Laura, helmets. Number and size." Beckett went on down the line, passing out clipboards. "Taylor, you've got the ascenders and cams, and I'll do ropes myself."

"Got it."

He pulled the first row of coiled ropes off the rack and dumped them on the table. Michael said they'd been checked at the end of last season, but Beckett wasn't letting anybody go up equipment he hadn't inspected himself, not even for the ridiculously easy climbs around here. As he unrolled the first coil and began checking the sheath, he noticed Taylor on her phone, frowning.

"Something wrong?"

Her head shot up. "What? No." She bobbled the phone and it bounced across the floor toward him.

He crouched to pick it up, automatically checking the screen for cracks. Not a one. "All hail the Otterbox." He handed it back to her, but not before he noted the Google search open to ascenders. He arched a brow.

Blushing, Taylor shoved the phone away. "Oh, I just remembered a particular one somebody told me about and was trying to remember what it was called."

She was lying. Right to his face, she was lying. That chapped his ass. He couldn't abide dishonesty. What he couldn't figure out was *why* she'd lie, so he let it go, keeping an eye on her through the rest of the inventory. It took a solid three hours before he was satisfied. As each of his people passed over their clipboard, he went over it, adding notations to a master list of equipment that needed to be replaced or retired. When he reached Taylor's list it confirmed his suspicions.

Disappointment flared through him, but Beckett said nothing, setting the clipboard aside. "Looks like y'all have a little extra time before dinner. Go make the most of it."

Everybody cheered. Taylor was at the head of the pack trying to get out of the shed.

"Taylor, stay back a minute? I wanted to go over some things."

Her foot hovered inches out the door before she turned back around, a too bright smile pasted in place. "Sure."

Shit.

He waited until everybody was considerably down the path, then shut the door. "We have a problem."

"We do?"

"You don't know your equipment. And if you've done more than go up the wall at the local gym, I'll go do a handstand at the top of Boulder Mountain."

Taylor just closed her eyes, resignation in every line of her body.

"How the hell did you get assigned to rock climbing?" Beckett demanded. "Did you lie on your application?"

"No. No, I—It's complicated."

He crossed his arms and waited. "Look, these may be relatively easy climbs, but I'm not having anybody out there who doesn't know what they're doing. That's dangerous to everybody involved. So you're either going to explain yourself, right now, or I'm headed to Michael and having you fired."

The blood drained from her face. "You have every right to be upset—"

"Damned right, I do."

"Look, I'll explain everything. Just not here. Will you come with me?"

Beckett frowned. "Where?"

"There's bound to be somewhere to eat in Briarsted. Let me buy you dinner and explain."

He couldn't imagine an explanation that was going to end in any other way but her being canned, but he'd liked her, so he could give her the chance to spin this away from camp. "I'll get my keys."

They ended up at Boone's—part tavern, part gas station, part general store, and just about the only thing on the road between Camp Firefly Falls and Briarsted, the nearest town. As it was a Sunday night and early at that, the place wasn't too busy. A handful of patrons filled booths or stood around the pool tables. Kansas played on the jukebox in the corner, and as she watched a waitress sashay by with a slice of pie a la mode, Sarah half expected to see Dean Winchester waiting in a corner. But the star from *Supernatural* wasn't hanging around with a cocky smile and a willingness to drive her away from her predicament in his '67 Impala. She'd have to find her own way out of this.

Her actual companion wasn't the friendly, easy-going guy she'd flirted with at the lake. Beckett's blue-gray eyes had chilled to flint since inventory. Sarah couldn't blame him. Nobody appreciated being lied to, and when it came down to it, he was the one responsible for the safety of both his staff and the campers those staff members would be working with. He had every right to be pissed.

Sarah didn't hesitate to order a beer. She figured she'd need it to get through this mess and explain it in such a way that Taylor still had a job to come back to. They remained silent, studying the menu, until the waitress returned. In honor of Dean, she ordered a cheeseburger. Once the waitress left, Sarah tipped her longneck back for a healthy swig, then wrapped her hands around the bottle, as if it were some kind of anchor. "I did not lie on my application."

"Really?" Beckett's sarcasm thudded on the table between them like a stone.

Sarah held in a wince. How to get through this without throwing Taylor under the bus? "The truth is, it wasn't my application." She lifted her gaze to meet his and found him staring, his own beer halfway to his mouth.

"How's that?"

Truth, she decided, *insofar as possible.* "I'm not Taylor Meadows."

"You're—" Evidently deciding he needed alcohol for the rest of this story, he drank deep. "Then who the hell are you?"

"Sarah. Her identical twin sister."

Beckett only blinked. "You're shitting me."

"Nope." To prove it, she pulled out her phone and found a recent picture of the pair of them. Taylor was a little leaner, definitely tanner, but otherwise, only someone who knew them could easily tell them apart.

He studied the picture for a long time, then turned that penetrating gaze on her. She wanted to squirm, but held still. He handed the phone back.

"Okay, so that's one part of the mystery solved. Now you want to tell me exactly *why* you're impersonating your sister?"

"Because she asked me to." Even as the words fell from her lips, she realized how lame they sounded.

His brows winged up. "This is a thing y'all do for each other on a regular basis? Having some fun, screwing with people?"

"No. Well, not since we were about twelve, anyway. And this one time in college when she forgot to renew her driver's license." *Shut up. You're not helping your case.*

"So why now?"

Why indeed?

To buy herself some time to think, Sarah took another pull on her beer. "She's caught in a difficult situation in the job she's leaving, one she's obliged to try and accommodate because of an even more difficult situation in her personal life."

"Meaning what exactly?"

Sarah told him the story of Jax and the untenable position Taylor was stuck in. Their food came somewhere in the middle of the tale, so they ate while she talked and he listened. Other than muttering a few choice curses about Taylor's ex, Beckett stayed quiet until she'd finished.

"That sucks for her, it really does. Why didn't she just call up Heather or Michael and talk to them about it?"

Sarah opened her mouth, closed it again. *Because that would have been the responsible, adulting thing to do.* "I didn't ask. She came to me for help."

"But you could've said no." His tone implied she should have.

"I told myself the same thing. Right up until I said 'yes.' The thing is, I can never say 'no' to bailing Taylor out."

"Why not?"

"I'm the oldest."

Beckett gave her a bland stare. "By how much?"

"Fifteen minutes, but sometimes it feels like fifteen years. I'm the responsible one who has her shit together. Kind of goes with the territory." Sarah realized that made her sister sound like a flake. "Not that Taylor is irresponsible. When it comes to safety for climbing or rafting or any of the other things she does, she's serious as a heart attack. It's the money management and, I guess you'd say, interpersonal stuff, where she has trouble."

He swiped his last French fry through ketchup and pointed it at her. "And yet you, with your shit together, are here doing certification training for something you're not qualified for?"

Now she did wince. "The only part I'm not qualified for is the rock climbing. And I *have* actually done some climbs that weren't in the gym. Taylor's taken me a few times, but since I started grad school, there hasn't been time. Look, Taylor knows the handbook backward and forward. She's certified in first aid, CPR, and a whole laundry list of other things you probably saw on her application. She absolutely *is* qualified to deal with the rock climbing, and she'll be back by the test on Friday in plenty of time to prove it."

Beckett's eyes narrowed. "So you're asking what, exactly?"

"I'm asking you not to blow the whistle."

"You're asking me to lie." The hard tone told her she'd lost this battle, but she made one last effort.

"I'm asking you to wait. She needs this job. More, she desperately *wants* this job, and she'll be great at it. And if, for whatever reason, she doesn't pass the certification tests, then whatever the consequences are, they're on her. I'm just asking you to give her a chance."

Shoving the plate away, he sat back and studied her, finally shaking his head. "I won't lie to Michael. I won't pretend the person I'm working with is qualified, when she's not."

Sarah's hope withered. She blew out a breath. "I understand. I had no right to ask you to cover for her. For us. I'll find the Tullys when we get back to camp and explain."

"No, you won't. You're going back to camp, and we're going back to that equipment shed. And I'm not letting you leave it until you can name everything in there, piece-by-piece. Then tomorrow morning, you'll be up with the sun to start all over again."

She stared at him. "Excuse me?"

"I won't lie. But I'll get you certification-ready myself."

For a long moment she simply sat in stunned silence. "Why would you do that?"

"Much as I disagree with what you're doing, I appreciate the motivation behind it. I get what it means for somebody to give you a chance when the odds are stacked against you. Add to that, I like you." His mouth snapped shut after the admission, a little like slamming the barn door after the horses had gotten out.

"Thank you. Truly. My sister and I will both owe you."

Beckett waved that way. "Not worried about that. Now finish your burger. We've got a lot of work to do."

Beckett was going to regret this. What the hell was he thinking, promising to certify an almost totally green climber by the end of the week? Irritation—with himself, with the situation, with her— made his movements jerky as he unlocked the equipment shed and let them inside.

You weren't thinking with your big boy brain.

Which was also ridiculous. She'd be gone in a week. Where did he think this was gonna go?

He blamed Michael and Heather and their absurdly infectious happiness. He blamed this place. Most of all, he blamed the fact that he couldn't bet against the underdog. He'd been one too often in his life, so he had sympathy for the real Taylor. And a helluva lot of respect for the sister who was willing to put herself out there trying to help her.

"Sit," he ordered.

She did, without complaint, waiting as he gathered up gear.

By the time he sat across from her at the work bench, he was calmer. "I'm not going to ask you what you already know. I'll teach you as I'd teach any novice."

"Okay."

He slipped into instructor mode, repeating the lecture he'd given so often to beginner classes in the past. He went over components, explained their purpose, showed how each worked together. Through it all, Sarah listened, intent. And when he asked her to repeat the details back, she did, without error.

"You're a good student."

"Ought to be. I've practically made a career of it."

That's right. She'd mentioned she was in grad school.

Beckett picked up one of the harnesses. "Now we're going to suit you up." As he took in her expression of alarm, he added, "Not to climb tonight. Just to show you proper harness fit and begin introduction to the knots you'll be using." He held it out so she could step into it.

Hesitating only a moment, she laid her hand on his shoulder for balance and slipped one leg through, then the other. Beckett rose and worked the harness up, which pulled her nearly flush against his body. He'd been in this position countless times before, but his blood had never begun to pump like this. Her hand was still on his shoulder and her pupils dilated wide, those Bambi eyes tempting him to dive in and drown.

"Where are you in grad school?" he blurted, pulling his attention back to the harness and reaching for the waist strap, threading it through the buckle on the first side with as much business-like efficiency as possible.

Her hand fell away. "Columbia. This time."

"This time?"

A little sheepish, Sarah shrugged. "Taylor and I share an inability to settle on a career. Her response has been to move from job to job, trying out this or that. Mine has been to collect degrees."

"An expensive thing to collect." Even state colleges were hella expensive these days, and he knew well enough the cost of Ivy League education. He was still paying his off.

"If you're a good enough student, you can get scholarships or assistantships to pay for it. I like learning things, so as long as I could stay in school without going into debt, I picked that. It seemed less scary than the real world. My sister says I'm a terrible bookworm."

She didn't fit his mental image of a bookworm. Then again, he hadn't been the typical MBA student either.

Beckett grabbed the other side of the waist strap and threaded it through the buckle, drawing it snug. "There shouldn't be room to fit more than a couple of fingers in." He demonstrated and immediately regretted it as his fingers pressed against the flat of her belly. Just a thin layer of cotton separated him from skin. Sarah hissed a breath. He started to apologize, but instead, his eyes tracked to her mouth. Her lips were pink and glossy. He wondered if she'd taste like the pale ale she'd been drinking at dinner.

"You're supposed to…to double back the straps," she said.

For a moment, his mind blanked because his hand was still on her and he could feel her warmth against the backs of his fingers. What were they talking about?

"And tuck them in the sleeve." Her throat worked as she swallowed.

The harness. He was fitting her for the harness.

Beckett cleared his throat. "Right. Good."

Dropping his gaze, he finished adjusting the rest of the straps, which just put him in close proximity with those excellent legs of hers. His fingers itched to touch and stroke, to find out if her skin was as soft as it looked. Jesus, if he was this rattled by being close to adjust her harness, how was he going to teach her the rest of it?

Straightening, he gave her harness a few tugs, checking the fit. It would just take one pull to haul her into him...

"This is a terrible idea."

Beckett didn't realize he'd spoken aloud until she said, "Probably. But we've established I don't run from terrible ideas."

His eyes came back to hers, deep and dark and steady. Neither of them was talking about the climbing. The air between them snapped taut, shuddering like a rope under too much strain.

"Are we going to talk about this?' he rasped.

"Do you *want* to talk?" There went her eyebrow, that little sign of the sass he liked so much.

"No." If they talked about it, one or both of them would probably come to their senses and this moment would disappear. Foolish as it was, he didn't want that.

Sarah laid a hand on his chest. "Neither do I."

To hell with it.

Beckett gave in, curling his hands around her harness and tugging her into him, until they softly collided, body-to-body. Her arms slid around his waist as she tipped her face up. Her mouth was soft, yielding beneath his on a sigh that fired his blood. Needing to touch her, he lifted a hand to cup her nape, stroking the silky skin there before angling her head so he could take the kiss a little deeper. On a sexy little moan, she rose up, opening for him. They hovered there at that delicious edge of thickening arousal, and then she dove.

She flooded his senses, the taste of her, the scent of her, wrapping around him, pulling him under, on a fast, reckless slide that burned through whatever sense remained. Blind and deaf to anything but her, Beckett shifted, backing her up until they bumped against the table. Mouth still fused with hers, he lifted her onto it. And Jesus, her legs were as soft and toned as he imagined. She wrapped them around him, locking them at his back.

He skimmed his hands beneath her shirt, spanning the heated skin of her back. Hers followed suit, tunneling beneath his t-shirt to skate up his chest. Well, who was he to deny a lady? He yanked it off and found her lips again, glorying in the delighted purr she made as she explored his pecs and shoulders. When those fingers dug into his shoulders, he growled, and nudged up her tank top to find her pert breasts. She arched into his hands, against his hips and he went half-mad, greedily swallowing down her whimpers of pleasure.

Before he could think—because thought had long since stopped—his hands went for the button of her shorts. And found straps instead.

Confused, Beckett hesitated, tearing his mouth away to see what the hell the impediment was. The harness. The damned climbing harness he'd *just* put on her himself.

"Call the locksmith," Sarah gasped.

Her eyes were huge, dark, and devastatingly aroused.

"Did you just quote *Men In Tights* to me?"

Breath still heaving, the corner of that kiss-swollen mouth curved. "Seems I did."

Beckett chuckled, dropping his brow to hers. The chuckle rolled into a full on whoop of laugher. "My God, you may be my perfect woman." Finding a thread of control somewhere in the humor, he tugged down her shirt and skimmed a thumb over her cheek. "But this is not the perfect setting."

Her smile was wry. "I suppose I got a little carried away."

"I'm not complaining, as I was right there with you. But your chastity belt of webbing probably saved us from crossing a line that shouldn't be crossed tonight."

Sarah sucked in a breath and let it out on a long sigh. "You're right. More's the pity."

"A pity indeed," he murmured as she slid off the table. Because he didn't care for the look of regret in her eyes, Beckett tipped her chin up and brushed a quick, soft kiss over her lips. "But hey, tomorrow's another day."

~

If Taylor's ass had not been on the line, Sarah would've packed up in the dead of night and driven back to New York out of sheer embarrassment. Without the fog of lust, she was mortified. She'd practically climbed Beckett like a tree, and if not for the harness and his own heroic restraint, she was pretty sure they'd have ended up naked on that table in the equipment shed. That was…appalling.

She didn't have issues with sex. She liked sex—or had in the dim, dark recesses of her memory when she'd last had it. But she wasn't in the habit of going to bed—or table—with men she barely knew. Okay, she'd *never* been so carried away that she'd been tempted by the nearest horizontal surface. Beckett Hayes packed quite the sexual punch. And dear God, those shoulders. Damn. The fact was, sex appeal aside, she *liked* Beckett. He was focused, dedicated, thoughtful, and he had a helluva laugh, when he cut loose. He interested her more than anyone or anything had in more years than she could count.

And you're leaving at the end of the week.

That made last night a terrible idea, exactly as he'd said before they'd mauled each other. It had been unquestionably mutual. Which was the only reason she managed to make herself turn toward the equipment shed a quarter after sunrise the next morning, instead of veering toward the parking lot.

The campus was silent but for the twitter of a few birds, who didn't respect the holy rule of coffee before noise. Lake Waawaatesi was still and smooth as glass, reflecting the watercolor sky. Even in her uncaffeinated state, Sarah could appreciate that it was gorgeous. Somehow, that made the insult of being up at this hour a little bit less harsh. When was the last time she'd been somewhere this peaceful? At home, she'd be waking— unwillingly— to street construction or the honk and hum of traffic. This was better. So she paused, firing off a few shots with her camera to capture the moment for home.

The light was already on inside the equipment shed. Bracing herself, Sarah pushed the door open. Beckett stood at the table, sorting through a bin of ascenders. No doubt he was rechecking her work from yesterday. A fresh wave of embarrassment hit, and with it came gratitude that he'd figured it out. If something was wrong with any of the equipment she'd been meant to inspect, she'd prefer it be discovered rather than someone getting hurt because of her arrogance.

He turned. The smile started in his eyes, more blue than gray this morning, spreading like sunrise to the lips she'd dreamed about. And that, too, was a lovely way to start the day.

"Mornin'," he said. "I brought coffee."

The sweetest three words in the English language.

Zeroing in on the to-go cups emblazoned with the camp logo, Sarah made a beeline across the room. "You might be my perfect guy."

She met his gaze as she lifted her cup, and suddenly that didn't feel like joking flirtation.

Ridiculous. It's just chemistry.

But it didn't feel like just chemistry as she leaned back against the table and remembered his lips and hands on her. Sarah crossed her legs at the ankles and cleared her throat. "So what's on the agenda this morning? Knots?"

"It can wait a few minutes. Drink your coffee and let your brain come online."

"Bless you." Maybe then her brain would catch up with her mouth and keep her from saying anything stupid. She sipped. "Do you regret last night?"

Coffee fail.

Beckett lifted a brow. "Do you?"

"I—" She opened her mouth. Closed it again. "Not exactly. I'm just embarrassed, I guess. I don't normally... It's been a while, and..."

He just stared at her, waiting.

Sarah's cheeks went tight and hot. "Never mind. Forget I asked. Pre-coffee brain can't be trusted."

Beckett added another ascender back to the bin. "I don't regret it, no. And I don't think we have anything to be embarrassed about."

She liked that he said "we." And yet...

Another ascender went into the bin. "You don't look like that made you feel any better."

"It did. It's just—" Sarah sighed. "We barely know each other."

Beckett nodded and stayed silent for a few moments, checking and clearing another two ascenders. "So what do you want to know? What's your minimum threshold of knowledge that will make you more comfortable with this?"

She laughed a little. "I don't know."

Abandoning the ascenders, he caged her against the table, planting his hands behind her. He didn't touch her, but Sarah was aware of every hard inch of him as he leaned in, close enough that it would barely take more than breathing to brush her mouth to his. He smelled of soap and cedar. Delicious.

"Look, I figure a spark like this doesn't come along every day. So, to my mind, it's worth following up to see if it fizzles or catches. So, what do you want to know?"

When you'll kiss me again. But that wasn't what he was asking. "I guess I can't say everything, can I?"

Beckett's lips curved, and he stepped back, returning to his bin of equipment. "Okay. I'll start with a mini-bio. I'm originally from Myrtle Beach, South Carolina. Non-smoker. Social drinker. Coke over Pepsi. Dogs over cats. Morning person, which I hope you won't hold against me. Did my undergrad at USC, then grad school at Dartmouth, where I met Michael and Heather."

"Dartmouth?"

"Eh, don't be impressed. I left before I graduated."

Getting into an Ivy League graduate program was an achievement unto itself. She knew. "What were you studying?"

"I was getting my MBA."

"Really? I would've imagined—I don't know—environmental science or something."

"That would've been a better fit." He finished one bin and grabbed another. "I could have stuck it out, I guess. I was in the last year."

Sarah couldn't imagine being so close to finished and not following through. "Why didn't you?"

"They're big on group work in MBA programs. I found out in the middle of a presentation that my partner had plagiarized his entire half of the project."

"Oh my God. Did your professor fail you, too?"

"Nope. He just said that kind of thing happened in the real world, and I needed to get over it."

Her mouth fell open. "You're kidding!"

"Wish I was. I figured if that was what the real, corporate world was like. I'd never be happy, and I wanted none of it. I walked straight out. Didn't even finish my half."

"Ballsy."

"The word my parents used was 'stupid'. But that was later. There's a trailhead for the Appalachian Trail about a mile from campus. I packed a bag and hit the trail. By the time I made it to Virginia, I'd decided the National Park Service was my next step."

He said it casually, as if hiking what had to be around three hundred miles, give or take, was no big deal.

"You said you were at Yosemite the last three years?"

"Yeah. Stints at Conagree, Shenandoah, and Hot Springs before that."

"So what are you doing here at Camp Firefly Falls? I'd think summer would be high season for a park ranger."

"It is. I'm not a park ranger anymore." Though his tone was easy, a muscle jumped in his jaw.

"I'm guessing that wasn't as easy a decision as leaving Dartmouth."

"No. The powers that be didn't much appreciate my hijacking the park's social media account to counter the blatantly false information about climate change being spread by those currently running our government."

"My friends and I followed all that. All the rogue Twitter accounts that popped up to counter the official park accounts are awesome."

"I wasn't behind those, though I know a bunch of folks who were."

"Modern day heroes seeing that the truth gets told, no matter the consequences."

Beckett grunted. "Don't romanticize it. That particular brand of heroism made it rather hard to pay the bills. That's how I ended up here. Michael did me a favor."

That must be the chance he'd been given.

God bless Michael Tully.

He put the second bin of ascenders back on the shelf and grabbed two lengths of rope. "What about you? You said you collected degrees."

"Oh, well, it's possible my parents—proud though they were of the first three—might also be veering toward a different descriptor of my pursuits at this point."

"Three?"

"Working on my fourth." When he went brows up in expectation she sighed. "I've got bachelor's degrees in psychology, art, and nutrition. Right now I'm finishing up my master's degree in neurobiology and behavior."

"One of these things is not like the other."

Sarah laughed. "I love photography. I really wanted to be a photographer when I was younger, but, sadly, I have zero desire to shoot weddings or be a photojournalist, and there's not really any other great way to make a living as a photographer. But I threw in as many photography classes as I could for fun all through under-grad. Enough that it gave me another degree."

"So the passion is neurobiology?"

Sarah thought of the thesis she was ready to set on fire. "I'm not sure 'passion' is the right word."

"You don't like it?"

"I'm not sure you like anything by the time you get halfway through your thesis. I think despising your topic is part of the graduate school process."

Beckett hummed a noncommittal noise. "So you finish your master's degree. Then what?"

She thought longingly of the cabin she was sharing for the week and wished she were going to be here longer. "A vacation would be nice, but a Ph.D. is the plan."

"More graduate school in a subject you just admitted you despise?"

"A career in research seems to demand it."

"Is a career in research what you want?"

The practiced answer she'd been giving her parents for years was hovering on the tip of her tongue. But this was a man who'd walked away from *Dartmouth*. "I don't know what I want. Not business. I don't like that any more than you do. But I'm kinda too far down this path to jump off." Lord knew, if she changed fields again, her parents might kill her, even if they'd long since stopped paying her way.

"It's never too late to jump off."

The idea of it was simply mind-boggling. "I'm not as brave as you."

"I think you're plenty brave. Look at what you're doing here for your sister."

"That's not brave. It's foolhardy, as we established yesterday."

"Still. Deciding to admit you're on the wrong path—if you are,"

188 | KAIT NOLAN

he qualified, "takes guts. It's not for me to say one way or the other. But seems to me if you're not happy doing it, if you don't get excited about going in to do the job or the class or whatever, you're probably not in the best field."

When was the last time she'd been *excited* about her studies? Her first semester probably. Before they put her through the hell classes meant to weed out those who couldn't hack it. She'd proved she could more than hack it, but everything since then had been a grind. Especially this last semester. But if she didn't stick with neurobiology, if she didn't go on for her Ph.D., then what the hell would she do with her life?

"This is way too heavy a conversation for this hour of the morning," she declared.

"Fair enough. It's time we got started anyway."

Sarah set her empty cup down. "Teach me, oh wise one. What are we doing today?"

"You're going to practice your knots, and then you're suiting up and we're going to practice falling."

As she watched him grab the equipment, she didn't think she needed any more practice doing that.

Beckett loved summer storms. To his mind, nothing beat a good thunderstorm for driving people inside and encouraging naps—or other horizontal activities. Not that Sarah was cooperating on either front, just now. She stood at the doorway to his cabin, looking out at the torrential downpour that had granted them an unexpected reprieve from all the hard work of the week. The other staff had mostly holed up at the big lodge for games. Those who hadn't were ensconced in their own cabins, making the most of their leisure. He knew what he'd rather be doing with his.

"Will you come sit down?"

"Are you sure we can't head down to the equipment shed? Do some more drills or something? I hate to waste practice time."

It could never be said that Sarah didn't take her tutelage seriously. "Honey, you've conquered Boulder Mountain and passed every demonstration and oral quiz I've thrown at you." She had, in fact, excelled at every single challenge he'd thrown her way. She was a natural. "You've earned a break. C'mere." Beckett patted the bed beside him.

With one last glance out at the rain, Sarah slipped off her sandals and flopped down on the mattress, frowning.

"That is not the expression of a woman happy to be in my bed."

Her lip quirked into a half smile as she gave him the side eye. "I'm sorry. I just can't settle. I'm worried about the certification."

Beckett stroked a hand down her arm and laced his fingers with hers. "You're not the one who has to take the test." It was as much a reminder for himself as for her. He didn't want to think about the fact that she'd be gone in a couple of days, and he'd be spending the summer seeing a woman with her face who wasn't her.

"Yeah, but I'm in it now. I have to finish the training, have to be ready."

"Just in case?"

On a sigh, she rolled toward him, snuggling against his chest. "Mostly just to prove that I can be."

"Because everything's a competition."

Sarah hummed in agreement.

Beckett couldn't wrap his head around that worldview. "Does it come from being a twin? This competitive streak? Were you and Taylor always trying to outdo each other growing up?"

"Some. But a lot of times the competition is with myself."

He tipped his head down to study her. "What are you trying to prove?"

She considered the question. "I don't know. When I was younger, I think some of it was to prove that I wasn't like Taylor.

That I could stick things out, finish stuff. Then I guess I got addicted to winning. I like knowing I can push myself to do better, be better."

"Admirable," he conceded. "But exhausting, I'd think."

"Sometimes."

Beckett shifted her closer, pleased when she tangled her legs with his. "I think there's a place for competition and sticktoitiveness. But it's not everything. Some things shouldn't be finished. Fights. Brussels sprouts. Things that don't make you happy."

Sarah folded her hands across his chest and propped her chin on them. "Didn't it bug you? Walking away from your MBA, when you were so close to done?"

He didn't even hesitate. "No."

"You didn't feel like you'd wasted that time and money?"

"Some," he admitted. "But I don't think I'd have realized it wasn't for me without doing it. So in that sense, it wasn't a waste. I loved working for the National Park Service."

"I'm sorry things turned out like they did." Sympathy shone in those big, doe eyes.

"Eh, it's a hard job. Harder than most people realize. People think it's all hiking and climbing and doing fun outdoors stuff. It's also rescues and being law enforcement and dealing with deaths and drugs and a million other things that happen under the surface, behind the scenes. I was headed toward burning out there, too." Another three years, maybe five, he'd have been ready to move on.

"So now what?"

"I don't know. That's what I'm here to figure out this summer."

"I envy that. Having time to breathe, to think."

Beckett tucked a lock of her dark hair behind her ear. "You could take the time." He wanted her to take it. He wanted her to take it here, enough that he was prepared to talk to Michael about hiring her on. But that was getting ahead of things.

"I have a very tight schedule to finish my thesis." She said it with the ease of a well-rehearsed excuse.

"The thesis for the degree you're not sure you like, to go on to the PhD you aren't sure you want."

Her expression turned mulish, and he knew he'd probably pushed too far. But there was so little time to convince her.

"I'm just saying—that's a lot of years to invest in something you're not passionate about." The idea of it made him shudder. Being trapped like that would kill him. Sarah wasn't him, but he could see the cost down the road of her stubborn insistence about finishing what she started. "What's the worst that could happen if you took the time to make sure it's what you really want?"

"If I don't roll on into the PhD program this fall, I might not get in. I might miss my chance."

"Did it ever occur to you that if you took the time and didn't get in after this, that maybe you're supposed to do something else?"

"What? Like fate or God intervening?"

"I don't know. Maybe. I just think the universe tends to set us on the right path, if we're paying attention. But it's easy to get distracted by other stuff instead of listening."

"And you're here to listen this summer."

"That's the plan."

Sarah frowned, clearly flummoxed by the idea. "How do you deal with not knowing what comes next?"

"I've learned patience." Though she was testing it. He'd been listening all week and knew what he thought was next, at least with her. But she wasn't on the same page. Not yet anyway.

"Not my strong suit," she admitted.

He'd pushed her far enough for one day. "Then how about distraction?"

"What did you have in mind?" She went brows up in faux innocence.

"I volunteer as tribute." Grinning, he rolled her beneath him and took her mouth.

"You ready for a real challenge?" Beckett asked.

Sarah eyed the rock face, already mapping the path of her ascent. Her heart began to thump. This was no Boulder Mountain. But Beckett wouldn't have brought her out here if he didn't think she could do it.

"Yeah, I'm ready."

They suited up, going through the checklist she'd learned by rote, checking and rechecking safety equipment and determinedly not talking about the fact that she was leaving tomorrow. Sarah didn't know what he'd said to the Tullys so that they could spend their last day together in the adjacent state park, but she wasn't about to complain. There was nowhere she'd rather be than right here with him.

Something else she was determinedly not thinking about.

"You take the lead. I'll be right behind," he said.

On a nod she started the safety protocol. "On belay?"

Beckett grinned. "On belay." He had her locked in and ready to catch.

"Climbing."

"Climb on."

With a deep breath, Sarah took her first step and began to climb. Beckett said little other than offering up praise here and there. She kept her focus on the mountain, on the next hand-hold and foot placement. It was, she thought, a kind of moving meditation. There was no room for anything else, and she loved it.

Halfway up the rock face, she realized she'd miscalculated. The shelf that had looked minimal from the ground jutted out far more than she'd thought. The crevice she needed to reach was a foot beyond her fingers. Legs beginning to cramp, she clung to her position.

Now what?

"You okay?" Beckett called.

"There's no handhold I can reach. I can't go forward."

"So you adjust. Work with what's around you. There are more directions than up and down."

Sarah widened her view, shifting to check out her options to either side. If she made it about fifteen feet to the left, it looked like the overhang was minimal, with ready handholds for her to get up and over. But she couldn't see what came next.

Either way, you can't stay here.

"Slack!" she called.

"Slacking."

"Watch me."

"Go ahead."

Decision made, she began edging her way to the side.

"Good call. Keep your focus."

Sweat trickled between her shoulder blades, but Sarah barely noticed. She kept her attention on just what was in front of her, shoving up with her legs, stretching out. Her muscles trembled with fatigue as she hauled herself over the shelf and kept on going.

Finish what you start, Meadows. Get to the end.

When she pulled herself over the lip at the top, she shrugged out of the small pack and simply rolled to her back and lay there, staring up at the wide expanse of cloud-dotted blue as her heart rate began to slow and her breath evened out.

Beckett wasn't far behind, flopping down beside her. "You're missing the best part."

"I'm thinking breathing is the best part. Or maybe the not supporting my weight part."

He reached over to haul her up to sitting and gestured to the view she hadn't even stopped to see. "*That* is the best part."

The world opened up, a panorama of greens stretching as far

as the eye could see. "Wow. It's beautiful. And worth every aching muscle."

"I'll rub your back, if you'll rub mine."

Sarah bumped her shoulder against Beckett's. "That's a deal. Thanks for bringing me up here."

This was not a view she got in the city. The thought of it made her throat ache, even as she pulled out her camera. Central Park was nice and all, but there were people—constantly people—everywhere. Could she really go back to that? Could she endure it for another four years? Maybe more?

"Hey, you did that climb all on your own. I was just here for backup."

"I thought I was going to have to use you for backup when I got to that shelf."

"So you ended up on a path that wasn't what you intended. You still got to the destination you needed in the end."

Sarah gave him the side-eye. "Are you getting philosophical on me, Beckett?"

"Maybe. Hard not to, looking at that." He nodded toward the view.

"Subtlety isn't your strong suit."

"I'm out of time for subtle. That is the unfortunate truth. You leave tomorrow."

"And you think that's a mistake."

"It's not for me to say whether it's a mistake. I just know I don't want you to go." He stroked a thumb across her cheek. "That spark didn't fizzle, Sarah."

No, it definitely hadn't. But was this pull she felt with him the real deal? Or was he just another challenge? Something she'd started and felt compelled to see to the end?

"How do you see this working? For better or worse, my sister gets here tomorrow to take her rightful place. There's no job waiting here for me, even if I was free to take it. Which I'm not. I'm going to finish my thesis. I'm going to finish my Master's degree. I cannot have come this far down that path and not finish. Not when I'm this close."

Beckett laced his fingers with hers. "And what about finishing what you started here? With me? Or is this week it? Are we at the end, when we've barely even begun?"

Sarah framed his face between her palms, searching the blue-gray eyes so steady on hers. "I don't want this to be the end. But I don't—"

He pressed a finger to her lips. "Just stop right there. I don't need to hear the but. It's enough for me to know you don't want to walk away."

"But how will we—"

"We'll figure it out."

It was the kind of loose, optimistic planning Taylor was so prone to. The sort that usually ended in a crash and burn. Much as she wanted to give things a chance to work with Beckett, she couldn't see how they possibly would. What chance did a neuropsych grad student, who lived in Brooklyn, and an ex-national park ranger, who didn't even know where he'd be at the end of the summer, have of meeting in the middle long enough to see if they had a shot?

But as she sat with him at the top of their immediate world, Sarah found she didn't want to think about it. Instead, she leaned forward to brush her lips over his, determined to make the most of what little time they had left.

Beckett checked his watch, calculating how much time they had left before someone—Sarah or Taylor herself—would have to be slotted into the rotation for certification testing. Not a lot. He and Sarah stood at the edge of the staff parking lot, well away from all the goings on. She paced restlessly from one edge to the other, agitated that her sister hadn't shown up when she'd promised.

Was Taylor going to show at all?

Sarah's bags were packed. She was all set to walk away, and he didn't know what he was going to do about it. He'd lain awake half the night, turning the problem over in his head, wondering if he could convince her to give long distance a shot. It wasn't ideal, but maybe...

Beckett opened his mouth to say so.

"Where *is* she?" Sarah demanded. "She texted me when her flight landed in Boston. She should be here by now." She pulled out her phone and glared at it before shoving it back into her pocket.

This was not the right time, and she wasn't in the right mood, but he was out of time waiting for the right anything. He stepped into the path of her pacing, hands coming up to cup her shoulders. "Breathe. She'll be here when she's here. You've got this covered. You made sure of that."

"I just knew something like this was going to happen." She vibrated with tension and nerves, staring at the entrance to the parking lot, as if that would make Taylor appear.

Not what he wanted her thinking about. "Sarah, look at me. Please."

She lifted those big doe eyes to his. "I don't want this to come crashing down on you and get you in any kind of trouble."

"I'm fine. That's not what I want to talk to you about."

"Okay."

He felt her attention really shift to him then and slid his hands down to take hers. He hoped that was enough. "I don't want today to be goodbye."

Regret twisted that pretty mouth. "I—"

"Just let me finish. I know you're headed back to Brooklyn, and I know you're writing your thesis this summer, but there's no reason we can't still see each other. It's only two and a half hours away. I get time off. You could come up for a visit between writing stints."

"You'd do that? Come to New York?"

"Yeah. We could see where this goes."

The excitement that lit her eyes quickly banked. "And in the fall?"

"I don't know yet. But at least by then we'd know if we want to pursue this further. Just…think about it, okay?"

The radio at his belt crackled and Michael's voice rolled out. "Beck, where are you? Time to get rolling here."

Eyes still on Sarah's, he picked it up and answered. "On my way."

"Looks like time's up." She glanced back at the parking lot. "Guess I'm taking the certification test."

"You're ready."

She grimaced. "Too bad it's not my job."

She sent a quick text to Taylor, then they walked hand-in-hand back to the lodge, where the Tullys were handing out the policies and procedures test. Michael took one look at them and smirked. Beckett accepted the test and flipped him off. There'd be something to explain later when he didn't have a thing going with the actual Taylor, but that could wait. They had to get through this stuff first.

The morning rolled on. They knocked out the written test, passed everyone through final First Aid and CPR certification, and stopped for a quick snack before smaller groups broke off for individual activity certification with the outside instructors who'd been brought in for that purpose. Beckett took his troops, along with Heather,Michael, and the certification instructor, to the equipment shed. No way around it. Sarah was doing the full certification now. Even if Taylor miraculously appeared, there was no easy way to swap them out.

One-by-one, each of them was asked to demonstrate knowledge of equipment. When her turn came, Sarah rolled through it as if she'd been doing it for years, reciting everything he'd taught her without batting an eye. Then they trooped, en masse to

Boulder Mountain for the practical demonstration. As he was already certified for far more challenging climbs than this, Beckett took his position up top to observe and intervene as necessary.

When her turn rolled around, Sarah started on lead, working seamlessly with Diego as he took the intermediate path up for his own top rope test. Once Diego was back on the ground, they swapped. The whole process went smoothly, and Beckett shot Sarah a grin as she reached the top.

"Nearly done," he murmured. "You're doing great."

"I'm just ready for this to be over."

They took the descent together.

"Now, for our last test of the day, each of you will be expected to demonstrate the ability to properly and immediately catch at least three simulated falls," Richard announced. "Beckett has volunteered to be our test dummy. Now who's first?"

"Me." Sarah stepped up immediately.

They went through the safety check and clipped in.

"Belay on?" he asked.

"On belay."

"Climbing."

"Climb on."

Because he could, and because he knew she was anxious to get this over with, Beckett took the ascent fast, mimicking some of the rookie mistakes his people were bound to encounter. She took the first two slips like a champ, stopping his descent exactly as she should. Beckett headed on up to the top for the long drop. He glanced below, judging the distance and pegging the location of the various members of the crowd. And he saw Sarah walking up the trail.

"Oh sh—"

He didn't have to simulate the fall this time. His fingers just went numb. He hurtled down for two, gut-churning seconds before Sarah—actual Sarah—shouted "Gotcha!" and caught him.

They both dangled for a bit, his weight having hauled her several feet up the rock face.

"You okay?" she called.

"Yep."

"Holy shit!" someone exclaimed. "There are two of them!"

Sarah just closed her eyes.

"Ready to lower," Beckett said.

After a brief hesitation, her voice came back, "Lowering."

Time for all of them to face the music.

This is where it all falls apart, Sarah thought as she strode behind the Tullys up to the office at the lodge.

She'd expected Taylor to just impersonate her until such a time as they could make the switch. Taylor was dressed in the pre-arranged identical t-shirt and khaki shorts. But she'd come right out and introduced herself, which caused a predictable hubbub among those gathered. So much for all Sarah's hard work this week. Taylor had asked to meet with the Tullys privately, before the owners could make the request themselves. And maybe that was good. She was clearly intent on taking responsibility for herself. But how were they going to explain Sarah's presence here?

Taylor interrupted her train of thought. "That was a nice catch back there."

In the second it took to do her job, she'd lost five years off her life seeing Beckett plummet like that.

"Didn't know you knew how to do that," Taylor added.

"I've had a good teacher. And anyway, it shouldn't have been me. Where the hell have you been?" Sarah hissed.

Taylor shot her an assessing look, clearly wondering who that teacher had been, but she answered the question. "They lost my luggage, so I had to stick around and file a claim. And then by the time I got to the car rental place, they'd fouled up my reservation. Then there was construction on the route from the airport...I'm sorry. I got here as soon as I could."

"Yeah well, I'm thinking it's too little, too late, now."

"It'll be okay," Taylor soothed.

Sarah doubted it.

Michael shut the door to the office and turned to them. "Okay, I think I'm well within my rights to ask what the hell is going on?"

"There's a very simple explanation for this," Taylor began.

Heather crossed her arms. "I'd love to hear it."

"I'm Taylor Meadows. The actual Taylor Meadows you hired. This is my sister, Sarah, who's been impersonating me this week."

The Tullys stared, giving them both the hairy eyeball even as they shared the sort of dumbfounded shock at the resemblance. Sarah shifted, wishing she could just sink through the floor. This sounded even worse than when she'd told Beckett.

Eventually Michael asked, "Why?"

"Because I was stuck out in Wyoming on my previous job, past when I thought I'd be finished, and I was going to miss orientation, so I asked her to fill in for me."

Heather narrowed her eyes. "And you were, what? Going to just swap out after the fact without telling anybody?"

"That was the original plan yes. I was supposed to be back to take all the certification tests myself, but I ran into travel difficulties."

Michael frowned. "And you're coming clean now, why?"

"Because it's the right thing to do. I should never have asked Sarah to step in for me. I should've come to you directly when the problem arose, even if it meant losing the job. And I realize I'm probably losing it anyway, but at least my conscience will be clear."

A part of Sarah wanted to cheer that her sister was taking responsibility. It was the adult thing to do. But did she have to do it like this? Because the likelihood that Sarah would be welcome here ever again was nigh on nil.

Maybe Beckett really meant what he said about coming to visit her in Brooklyn.

Please let him have meant it.

She sighed. "Listen, I'm sorry for the deception. I was just trying to do her a favor."

Heather pinched the bridge of her nose. "I should have had more coffee this morning."

"You and me both," Sarah muttered. "Unless there's anything else?" She started toward the door. "My bag is already packed. I'll get off the premises immediately."

If she was lucky, maybe they'd give her a chance to say goodbye to Beckett.

Before she could cross the room, a brisk knock sounded and the door swung open without invitation. Beckett barged in. "Don't make any rash decisions."

Presumably he was speaking to the Tullys, but his eyes zeroed straight in on Sarah.

"Yes, Beck, please join the discussion," Michael said drily.

"Sorry. But I have something to say."

The determined glint in his eyes had Sarah stepping toward him. "Beckett, don't."

The last thing she wanted was him falling on his metaphoric sword for her and losing *his* job.

He just shot her an *I've got this* wave. "I know this is a weird situation, but I didn't want y'all tossing anybody out without listening. This isn't on Sarah."

Heather went brows up. "Wait, you knew she wasn't Taylor?"

"I figured it out pretty fast."

"And you chose *not* to turn her in," Michael confirmed.

"I did." Beckett's jaw firmed. "You're the one who kept spouting off about Pinecone Lodge."

Huh?

202 | KAIT NOLAN

Whatever that was about clearly meant something to the Tullys. Michael swore and Heather straightened, coming to very focused attention.

"Please don't take anything out on Beckett," Sarah insisted. "None of this was his idea."

That chiseled jaw turned to granite. Stubborn through and through. "Training you was my idea. And I stand by it. You can do the job. You just proved that."

"By rights we should fire the lot of you," Michael said. "This whole thing could be an insurance nightmare."

"Nobody got hurt," Beckett insisted. "And Sarah passed all the certifications."

"Not the point. The job wasn't hers."

"Michael," Heather chided. "We've already lost two instructors, one to a broken leg, the other to a family emergency. And our nutritionist up and eloped to Bora Bora. We can't afford to lose more. Beckett, you're not going anywhere. And Taylor, as long as you actually pass the certifications, you can stay."

"Thank you. Seriously," Taylor gushed. "That's more than I was expecting."

"What about Sarah?" Beckett asked.

"What about her? She's not in any kind of trouble," Heather said. "What would we charge her with? Conspiracy to do a good job? She aced everything."

"Of course, she did," Taylor muttered, but she softened it with a grin.

"You said you lost your nutritionist," Beckett interrupted. "Sarah has a degree in nutrition."

Heather's gaze sharpened. "Really?"

"Just a bachelor's degree. I'm not licensed or anything."

"But you could probably handle coordinating with the chef and her staff to deal with any special dietary restrictions of guests, right?" Heather pressed.

"Well, yeah, that's easy. But—"

"We could use you," Michael admitted.

Sarah's head spun. Work here? Stay the summer? She looked to Beckett.

He angled his head. "Different path."

"I still have to finish my thesis by the end of the summer."

"Yeah, but think about it, Sarah. You said you were having trouble writing in Brooklyn. The guests wouldn't take up *that* much of her time, would they?" Beckett asked, turning to Michael.

"Some sessions more than others, but no, it wouldn't be that bad. We might ask you to pinch hit occasionally, but it certainly wouldn't be a problem for you to write around that."

"You'd have time to write up here. Time and quiet," Taylor pointed out. "And plenty of fodder for your camera."

And Beckett. I could have Beckett.

Sarah didn't know what she wanted for a career. She didn't know if she really wanted her PhD. She didn't know if she'd change her mind about the path she was on. But she knew she wanted more than this week with him.

She let the smile come, and warmed as she watched the matching curve of Beckett's lips. "Then I guess I'm here for the summer."

When he stretched out his hand, she took it.

"I told you we'd figure it out," he said.

"So you did." Sarah moved into him, pressing her cheek to his chest as he wrapped his arms around her. All the tension she'd been carrying around for the past week simply drained out of her. Taylor would, no doubt, be looking for explanations, but that could wait. Right this second, she just wanted to stand here and bask.

The digitized camera noise had her lifting her head in time to see Michael lining up for another shot with his phone.

"Look over here and smile now. For the bulletin board at Pinecone Lodge."

~

Beckett set his feet for the last climb of the day. Frasier, a CPA out of California, who'd come with his husband for Grease Week, had decided to branch out from the musical-themed activities for something a little more outdoorsy. Of course, the rest of the Pink Gaydies had come to watch. Tavi, Harley, and Everett—Frasier's more outgoing half—stood back from Boulder Mountain shouting encouragement.

"You've got this, honey!"

"Piece of cake."

"That harness does amazing things for your ass," Everett said.

"I'm much more concerned with how well it keeps my ass from falling off the mountain," Frasier shot back.

"You're all tied in properly," Beckett assured him. "Anything happens, I'm right here to catch you."

"With all those muscles, you can catch *me* anytime," Tavi announced.

Beckett held in a snort. These guys had been some of the most entertaining campers of the summer.

"Too late," Taylor interjected. "He got caught months ago by my sister."

"Who should have been back by now," Beckett groused.

Sarah had left yesterday for New York. Her thesis defense had been scheduled for nine o'clock this morning. Even with the expectation that the defense could take a few hours, he'd expected to hear from her by lunchtime about how it went. Now it was coming up on dinner. Even taking into account the spotty cell service up here, she should have been back to camp. The lack of word was making him twitchy. What if the familiarity of academia had her jumping at the PhD program?

"Relax. She probably had lunch with her committee and then stopped by her apartment in Brooklyn on her way out of town. It's Friday. Traffic getting out of the city will be a bitch."

Taylor was probably right. But he'd feel better once he laid eyes on her himself.

"You ready, Frasier?" Beckett asked.

"Belay on."

"On belay."

Frasier made his climb with minimal trouble, only losing his footing once and catching himself before Beckett had to intervene. By the time he headed off with the rest of the Pink Gaydies for evening drinks at the boathouse, he was enjoying the rank of conquering hero.

Beckett began checking and coiling the ropes.

"I'm sure she's fine," Taylor assured him.

He only grunted.

"Beck."

In the expectant silence, he lifted his eyes to Taylor's—eyes the same color and shape as Sarah's, but with a sharpness he'd learned to recognize over the summer.

"She's crazy about you. She didn't change her mind."

He sure as hell hoped not because he was all in with Sarah. Not pressing these past couple of months had been one of the hardest things he'd ever done. But Beckett knew she had to come to a decision on her own or she'd always doubt herself. "Guess we'll see."

They hauled equipment back to the shed and stowed it.

"I'm headed up to the boathouse. You coming?" Taylor asked.

"Nah. I'm headed back to my cabin, grabbing a shower. See you at dinner, maybe."

As she headed on up the trail, someone knocked on the doorframe. Beckett whipped around, expecting to see Sarah. The balding guy in the doorway was a severe disappointment. Shaking off his mood, Beckett worked up a smile. "Hey Trent. How was the hike today?"

"A welcome relief from all the fifties-themed everything. I love my wife, but dear God, a man can only take so much."

Beckett's lips twitched. Trent Cunningham had given his wife this week at camp for an anniversary present because *Grease* was her favorite movie. He hadn't realized exactly how hard-core the theme would be when he agreed to come along. In between all the dance classes, fifties makeovers, and karaoke, he'd ended up spending every day in Beckett's neck of the woods, climbing, ziplining, and hiking in the nearby state park. Beckett liked the guy.

"Looking for more escape activities for tomorrow?" Beckett asked.

"No, actually. I wanted to talk to you about something."

"All right. Come on in."

Trent made himself at home, sitting at the table. "I had a chat about you with Michael Tully today."

Beckett frowned. "Why?"

"Because I wanted to see if his impression of you matched mine. And it does. He gave you a glowing recommendation."

"Recommendation for what, exactly?"

Trent smiled. "I'm getting ahead of myself. I'm CEO of The Balanos Society. We're a non-profit dedicated to wilderness conservation."

The name was familiar. Beckett wracked his brain. "Out of… North Carolina?"

"Yeah. We're based in Raleigh, though we've got projects stretching through most of the Appalachian Trail. We're spearheading some of the efforts toward reforestation in the Gatlinburg area after the fires down there. It's a big job, and we could use someone who can liaise with the National Park Services and other key stakeholders in the area. Someone with experience in that world, who would also be qualified to get out and get his hands dirty on site to document progress of the project. I think you'd be great in that role."

Beckett stared at him. "You're offering me a job?"

"Yeah. We're in early stages of the project, and there are

numerous positions to fill, but I'd love to get you in on the ground floor. You interested?"

"I'd certainly like to hear more about it."

Trent filled him in, and the more Beckett heard, the more the thought this job was tailor-made just for him. But he wasn't thinking just about himself now.

"You said you wanted someone to document progress of the project. What kind of documentation are you talking? Photographs? Reports?"

"Definitely. We want pictures of the efforts we're making and also documentation of what survived."

"So, might you have a position for a full-time photographer? Or a position that's predominantly photography with room to expand into other areas with training?"

Trent's gaze sharpened. "You've got someone in mind."

"I do. And she's damned good."

Before he could say more, the shed door flew open and Sarah danced through. "I *passed!*" She did a victory boogie before realizing Beckett wasn't alone. She laughed. "Sorry about that. I've been celebrating for the past few hours. I just passed my master's thesis defense. My degree shall be conferred in October, and I am officially *done with school.*"

"*Done* done?" Beckett asked.

"I shall not be gracing Columbia's campus this fall," she announced. "God knows what I'll be doing instead, but you were right. That PhD was not going to make me happy." She slipped an arm around him and rose to her toes to brush a quick kiss over his lips. "But you do."

Trent divided a glance between them. "The photographer?"

"Yeah."

"Say what now?" Sarah asked.

Beckett wrapped his arms around her. "How do you feel about Tennessee?"

"I don't know. I've never been. Well, unless you count layovers at the Memphis airport."

"I've got a project down there," Trent said.

Sarah listened as he gave the rundown. Though her expression remained neutral, the hand curved around Beckett's waist tightened with every word. "Let me get this straight. You've got a job for me as a photographer?"

"For documentation, yes. And prospectively promotional materials if you're as good as Beckett says you are."

Her brow furrowed, and Beckett could almost see the wheels turning in her head. "I assume something like this would be time limited?"

"We envision this particular project taking two to five years. But the organization itself continues to grow. We have conservation projects all over the eastern US. Provided things worked out all around, there's the potential for longer-term careers." Trent straightened. "I don't need an answer right away. I just wanted to put a bug in your ear. Think about it, and let me know. Meanwhile, I'll leave you two to your celebrating. Congratulations on your successful defense."

Then they were alone.

Sarah pulled away and sagged against the table. "Wow. That was...entirely unexpected."

"It's a lot to hit you with right when you get back," Beckett admitted. "But what do you think?"

"I think this job is perfect for you. It takes the eco-conservation stuff you loved from the park service and moves it to center stage."

"What about you? It's a shot at actually being a professional photographer. I mean, it's not all pretty landscapes and stuff, but it's not people."

"I never even thought about photography being a legitimate career path. And here you've taken the thing I really love and come up with a job option that would pick up almost as soon as

I'm out of contract here. One that means I don't have to choose between doing what's practical and being with you."

"I didn't so much come up with it as have it fall into my lap. But it's an option. One we didn't have yesterday."

Eyes on his, Sarah shoved away from the table. "Maybe it's what I'm supposed to do. Maybe not." She laced her hands behind his back and pressed close. "But if the Universe is trying to tell me something, I'm listening."

WHEN YOU GOT A GOOD THING

THE MISFIT INN, BOOK #1

Charming, poignant, and sexy, *When You Got a Good Thing* **pulled me in with its sweet charm and deft storytelling, and didn't let go until the very last page. It has everything I love in a small-town romance!** ~USA **Today Best-Selling Author Tawna Fenske**

She thought she could never go home again. Kennedy Reynolds has spent the past decade traveling the world as a free spirit. She never looks back at the past, the place, or the love she left behind —until her adopted mother's unexpected death forces her home to Eden's Ridge, Tennessee.

Deputy Xander Kincaid has never forgotten his first love. He's spent ten long years waiting for the chance to make up for one bone-headed mistake that sent her running. Now that she's finally home, he wants to give her so much more than just an apology.

Kennedy finds an unexpected ally in Xander, as she struggles to mend fences with her sisters and to care for the foster child her mother left behind. Falling back into his arms is beyond tempting, but accepting his support is dangerous. He can never know the truth about why she really left. Will Kennedy be able to bury the past and carve out her place in the Ridge, or will her secret destroy her second chance?

Chapter One

"*W*ELCOME TO O'LEARY'S PUB. What can I get you?" The greeting rolled off Kennedy Reynolds' tongue as she continued to work the taps with deft hands.

The man on the other side of the long, polished bar gaped at her. "You're American."

Kennedy topped off the pint of Harp and slid it expertly into a patron's waiting hand. "So are you." She injected the lilt of Ireland into her voice instead of the faint twang of East Tennessee. "You'd be expectin' somethin' more along these lines, I'd wager. So what'll it be for a strapping Yank like yourself?"

The guy only blinked at her.

So she wasn't exactly typical of County Kerry, Ireland. Her sisters would be the first to say she wasn't exactly typical of anyone, anywhere. It didn't bother her. But there was a line stacking up behind this slack-jawed idiot, and she had work to do.

"Can I suggest a pint of Guinness? Or perhaps you'd prefer whiskey to warm you through? The night's still got a bit of a chill."

He seemed to shake himself. "Uh, Jameson."

She poured his drink, already looking past him to take the next order, when he spoke again.

"How's a girl from—is that Texas I hear in there?—wind up working in a pub in Ireland?"

This again? Really? Kennedy repressed the eye roll, determined to be polite and professional

A big, long-fingered hand slapped the guy on the shoulder

hard enough to almost slosh the whiskey. "Well now, I suppose herself walked right in and answered the help wanted sign." The speaker shifted twinkling blue eyes to Kennedy's. "That was how it happened in Dublin, now wasn't it, darlin'?"

"And Galway," she added, shooting a grin in Flynn's direction. "I'd heard rumor you were playing tonight. Usual?"

"If you'd be so kind. It's good to see you, *deifiúr beag*." His voice was low and rich with affection, the kind of tone for greeting an old lover—which was laughable. Flynn Bohannon was about as far from her lover as he could get. But it did the trick.

With some relief, Kennedy saw the American wander away. "Thanks for that."

"All in a day's work," Flynn replied.

"I've missed your pretty face." She glanced at the nearly black beard now covering his cheeks as she began to pull his pint of Murphy's Irish Stout. "Even if you are hiding it these days."

He grinned, laying a hand over his heart. "Self preservation, love."

"You keep telling yourself that." Kennedy glanced at the line snaking back through the pub. "I'm slammed here, and you're starting your set shortly. Catch up later?"

Flynn lifted the beer and toasted her before making his way toward the tiny stage shoehorned beside the fireplace, where the other two members of his trio were waiting.

Mhairi, one of the waitstaff, wandered over, setting her tray on the bar as she all but drooled in his direction. "Well now, I'd not be kickin' that one out of bed for eating crisps."

"Wait 'til you hear him play."

Mhairi glanced back at Kennedy, lifting a brow in question. "Are you and he…?"

"No. Just friends. The way there is clear, so far as I know."

The waitress smiled. "Brilliant." She reeled off orders and it was back to the job at hand.

As Kennedy continued to pour drinks, Flynn and his band tuned instruments. They weren't the same pair who'd been with him in Dublin, whom she'd traveled with for several weeks as an extra voice. That wasn't much of a surprise. It'd been—what?—a year or so since they'd parted in Scotland. Flynn would, she knew, go where the music took him. And that sometimes meant changing up his companions. He was as much an unfettered gypsy as she was, which was why they'd become such fast friends. But whereas he didn't mind a different city or village every night, she preferred to take a more leisurely pace, picking up seasonal work and staying put for two or three months at a stretch. Really immersing herself in the culture of a place. The ability to pause and soak in each new environment gave her both the thrill of the new and kept her from feeling that incessant, terrified rush of not being able to fit in everything she wanted to see or do. It was important to her to avoid that, to take the time to be still in a place and find out what it really had to teach her.

The itinerant lifestyle worked for her. She'd seen huge chunks of the world over the past decade, made friends of every stripe, picked up bits and pieces of more than a dozen languages. Many people saw her life as unstable. She preferred to think of it as an endless adventure. What did their stability give them? Consistent money in the bank, yes. But also boredom and stress and a suffocating sameness. No, thank you. Kennedy would take her unique experiences any day. Never mind that the desk jobs and business suits had never even been a possibility for her. She'd been ill-suited for the education that led to those anyway.

Across the pub, Flynn drew his bow across his fiddle and launched into a lively jig. The crowd immediately shifted its focus. Those who knew the tune began to clap or stomp in time, and a handful of patrons leapt up and into the dance. Kennedy loved the spontaneity of it, the unreserved joy and fun. As jig rolled into reel and reel into hornpipe, she found herself in her own kind of dance as she moved behind the bar. Flynn switched instruments with the ease of shaking hands, playing or lifting his voice as the tune dictated. He even dragged Kennedy in for a couple of duets that made her nostalgic for their touring days. His music made the night pass quickly, so she didn't feel the ache in her feet until she'd shut the door behind the last patron.

Flynn kicked back against the bar. "A good night, I'd say."

"A very good night," Kennedy agreed.

"Help you clean up?"

"I wouldn't say no."

They went through the motions with the other staff, clearing tables, wiping down, sweeping up. Mhairi went on home—disappointed. And Kennedy promised Seamus, the pub's owner, that she'd lock up on her way out. Then, at long last, she settled in beside the remains of the fire with her own pint.

Flynn lifted his. "To unexpected encounters with old friends."

"Why unexpected?"

"You said yourself you rarely stay more than three months in a place. You've already been from one coast of Ireland to the other. I didn't expect you back."

"I always seem pulled back here," she admitted. "The people. The culture. As a whole, I suppose Ireland has been as close as I've had to a home base over the past ten years. I've spent more collective time in this country than anywhere else combined since I started traveling."

"How long have you been in Kerry?"

"Coming up on three months."

"Thinking of settling?" he asked.

Was she? No. She still felt that vague itch between her shoulder blades that she got every time she'd been long enough in a place. She knew she'd be moving on soon, searching for the next place to quiet the yearning she refused to acknowledge. "Not exactly. I haven't decided where I want to go next. Which isn't the same thing." She took a breath and spilled out the news she'd told no one. "I've been contacted by a book editor in New York. She wants me to turn my blog into a book."

"Really?" Flynn's grin spread wide and sparkling as the River Liffey. "That's grand!"

It was the most exciting thing to ever happen to her, and she was glad to finally get a chance to share it. "I haven't said yes."

"Why not? Are the terms not to your liking?"

"We haven't gotten that far. I'm still thinking about it." Still looking for reasons to talk herself out of it.

"What's there to think about?" Flynn prodded.

"A book means deadlines and criticism and working on other people's schedules. None of those are exactly my strong suit."

"Bollocks. Every job you've had has been on someone else's schedule. As to deadlines, how hard can it be to take what you've already written and turn it into a book? *Not All Who Wander* is well-written, engaging, and personal. You're a talented writer."

On her better days, Kennedy could admit that. But it was one thing having her little travel blog, with its admittedly solid online following, be read and commented on via the anonymity of the internet. It was a whole other animal turning that into a book that lots of people could read. Or not read, as the case might be. That was opening herself up to a level of failure she didn't even want to contemplate.

"She's offered to fly me to New York to meet with her, and I'm thinking about taking her up on the offer. I might feel better about the idea of the project if we talk about it in person."

"And if you go back across the pond, will you finally take a detour home?"

At the mention of Eden's Ridge, Kennedy felt some of her pleasure in the evening dim. "It hasn't really been on my radar as an option."

"Maybe it should be."

She lifted a brow. "This from the man who's been on the go nearly as long as I have?"

"I travel and often, yes, but I've been home. I've seen my family. You've been running."

"I'm not running," she insisted.

"All right, not running. Searching, then. For something. In all your travels, have you found it?"

"How can I even answer that? I don't know what I'm looking for." But that was a lie. She knew what she was looking for and knew she wouldn't find it in any new country, on any new adventure.

"I'd say that's an answer in and of itself."

Kennedy scowled into her beer. "I've had my reasons for staying away from home."

"They aren't family. You've seen them since you left. So who?"

Her gaze shot to his.

Flynn jerked his shoulders and gave an easy smile. "Deduction, *deifiúr beag*. Who was he?"

Someone better off without me.

She was saved from answering by the ringing of her mobile phone. "Late for a call." Fishing it out of her pocket, she saw her mother's number flash across the screen. "Not so late back in Tennessee." She hit answer. "Hey, Mom."

"Kennedy."

At the sound of her name, she felt her stomach clench into knots. Because it wasn't her mother, and the strain in her eldest sister's voice was palpable. "Pru?"

"Are you sitting down?"

Absolutely nothing good could follow those words. "What?"

Beside her, Flynn straightened, setting his pint to the side.

"You're not on the street where you can accidentally walk into traffic or something are you?"

"I'm sitting. What the hell is going on? Where's Mom?"

Her sister took a shaky breath. "Kennedy, Mom was in an accident. Her car was in the shop, and she was in a loaner. We've had a cold snap."

"What?" Kennedy whispered.

"She…" Pru gave a hiccuping sort of sob. "She didn't make it"

The earth fell out from beneath Kennedy's chair, and she curled her hand tighter around the phone, as if that pitiful anchor would help. She didn't even recognize her own voice as she asked, "Mom's dead?"

She wasn't aware of Flynn moving, but suddenly he was there, his strong hand curling around hers.

"The doctors said it was all but instant. She didn't suffer. I…we need to make arrangements."

"Arrangements." She needed to get the hell off the phone. She needed to move, to throw something, to rail at the Universe because this…this shouldn't be happening. "I have to go."

"Kennedy, I know this is hard but—"

"I'm coming home. I'll be there absolutely as soon as I can. Call you back as soon as I know when." She hung up before Pru could answer.

"Do you want me to come with you?" Flynn asked.

He would. He'd cancel whatever bookings he had and fly across an ocean with her to face the grief and demons that waited in Eden's Ridge But this was for her to do.

"No. I… No." Lifting her eyes to his, she felt the weight of grief land on her chest like a boulder. She'd never again hear her mother's laugh. Never smell her mother's favorite perfume. Never get a chance to tell her the truth about why she'd walked away. "Flynn."

Without word, without question, he tugged her into his arms, holding tight as the first wave crashed over her, and she fell apart, the phantom scent of violets on the air.

∽

CHIEF DEPUTY XANDER KINCAID parked his cruiser in front of the rambling Victorian that had been Joan Reynolds' home. He retrieved the covered dish of chicken enchiladas sent by his mama —the first wave of death casseroles that would soon fill the old kitchen to bursting—and headed for the front door. Despite its size, with its muted gray paint, the house tended to blend into the woods and mountains around it. Joan had loved this house. She'd always said it was a peaceful spot, a good place to heal and a good place to love. And she'd done exactly that for nearly twenty-five of her sixty-two years, filling the over-sized house with foster children who'd needed a home and someone to love them.

No telling whose home it would become now. Pru had moved back in. As the only one of Joan's adopted girls who hadn't moved away, she'd immediately stepped in to take over guardianship of Ari Rosas, Joan's most recent—well, her last foster child. But he didn't imagine Pru could afford the upkeep of the place on her income as a massage therapist—especially after the death taxes and probate lawyer had their way with the place. And what, he wondered, would happen with Ari, whose adoption hadn't yet been finalized?

Juggling the casserole dish, he rang the bell and waited. And waited.

Backing up on the porch, he craned his head to peer around toward the barn. Pru's car was there. He tried the knob and found it unlocked. Making a mental note to have a word with her about security, even here on the Ridge, he stuck his head inside. "Pru?"

She appeared at the head of the stairs, her big brown eyes red-rimmed from crying. "Sorry. I was just..." She tailed off, waving a vague hand down the hall.

"It's fine." He lifted the enchiladas. "Mama wanted me to bring these by. She thought with your sisters coming in, the last thing you or any of them would want to do is cook."

Xander watched as manners kicked in. Her posture straightened, her expression smoothing out as she locked down the grief.

"That's so kind of her." She came down the stairs and reached for the dish. "I'll just go put this in the kitchen."

He followed her back.

"No one's here just yet," she said, a false bright note in her voice, as if everything was fine and her world wasn't falling apart.

Xander waited until she slid the casserole into the fridge before he simply wrapped his arms around her. "Pru. I'm so sorry."

For a long moment, she stood there like a wooden post. Then a shudder rippled through her as her control fractured. Her arms lifted and she burrowed in.

"This shouldn't have happened," she whispered. "If she'd been in her own car instead of that tin can loaner, it wouldn't have."

Xander wasn't sure Joan's SUV would've handled the patch of black ice any better, but he remained silent. The fact was, nobody expected black ice in east Tennessee in March. Not when daytime temperatures were almost to the sixties. Joan's hadn't been the only accident this week. But she'd been the only fatality.

He ran a hand down Pru's silky, dark brown hair, hoping to soothe, at least a little. But this wasn't like middle school, when he'd been able to pound Derek Pedretti into the ground for making Pru cry by calling her fat. There was no one he could take to task, no one to be punished. Grief simply had to be endured.

"There are all these arrangements to be made," she hiccupped.

And no one here to help her do them, with Maggie off in Los Angeles and Athena running her restaurant in Chicago. Xander deliberately avoided thinking about the final Reynolds sister, though he was sure that this would bring even her home. The idea of that caused his gut to tighten with a mix of old fury and guilt.

"What can I do to help?"

"Let me make you some coffee."

"Pru—"

"No really," she sniffed, pulling away. "I'm better when I'm doing something."

Xander didn't want coffee, but if she needed to keep her hands busy, he'd drink some. "Coffee'd be great."

She began puttering around the kitchen, pulling beans out of the freezer and scooping them into the grinder. Joan had loved her gourmet beans. It'd been one of the few luxuries she'd always allowed herself. As she went through the motions, Pru seemed to regain her control.

"Maggie's taking the red eye from LA, and Athena's flying out as soon as she closes down the restaurant tonight."

"Do either of them need to be picked up from the airport?"

"They're meeting in Nashville and driving up together in the morning, so they'll be here to help me finish planning the service. It's supposed to be on Thursday."

Xander didn't ask about Kennedy. Both because he didn't want to care whether she showed up, and if she wasn't coming, he didn't want to rub it in.

Pru set a steaming mug in front of him, adding the dollop of half and half he liked and giving it a stir. "Kennedy gets in day after tomorrow. There was some kind of issue getting a direct flight, so she's having to criss-cross Europe before she even makes it Stateside again. She's coming home, Xander."

He wasn't sure if that was supposed to be an announcement or a warning, but it cracked open the scab over a very old wound that had never quite healed.

She laid a hand over his. "Are you okay?"

This woman had just lost her mother, and she was worried about whether he'd be okay with the fact that his high school girl-friend, whom he hadn't seen in a decade, was coming home.

"Why wouldn't I be?"

Pru leveled those deep, dark eyes on his. "I know there are unresolved issues between you."

God, if only she knew the truth—that he was the reason Kennedy had left—she wouldn't be so quick to offer sympathy.

"It was a long time ago, Pru. There's nothing to resolve."

Kennedy had made her position clear without saying a word to him. At the memory, temper stirred, belying his words. There were things he needed to say to her, questions he wanted answered. But whatever her faults, Kennedy had just lost her mother, too, and Xander wasn't the kind of asshole who'd attack her and demand them while she was reeling from that. Chances were, she'd be gone before he had an opportunity to say a thing. He'd gotten used to living with disappointment on that front.

He laid a hand over Pru's. "Don't worry about me. How's Ari?"

She straightened. "Devastated. Terrified. And..." Pru sighed. "Not speaking."

"Not speaking?"

"Not since I told her. She'd come so far living here with Mom, and this is an enormous setback. No surprise. Especially having just lost her grandmother last year." Pru continued to bustle around the kitchen, pouring herself a cup of coffee and coming to sit with him at the table. Her long, capable fingers wrapped around the mug.

"She upstairs?"

"Yeah. I was trying to get her to eat something when you got here."

"Poor kid. Have you talked to the social worker yet?"

"Briefly. Mae wants to let us get through the funeral and all the stuff after before we all figure out what to do."

"Who would've been named her emergency guardian if the adoption had gone through?" Xander asked.

"The four of us, probably. I know it's what Mom would've wanted. But there are legal ramifications to the situation, and the fact is, I'm the only one still here." She sighed. "We'll have to talk about it after. The one thing I know we'll all be in agreement on is that we want what's best for Ari."

"All four of you have been in her shoes, and you turned into amazing women. I know you'll do the right thing." Whatever that turned out to be.

Xander polished off the coffee. "I'm on shift, so I need to be getting back. But, please, if you need *anything*, Pru, don't hesitate to call. I'm just down the road."

She rose as he did and laid a hand on his cheek. "You're a good stand-in brother, Xander. Mom always loved that about you."

He felt another prick of guilt, knowing his own involvement with this family had been heavily motivated by trying to make up for Kennedy's absence. "Yeah well, I ran as tame here as the rest of you when we were kids. Especially when Porter was around." Giving her another squeeze, he asked, "Can I do that for you? Notify the rest of her fosters? I know you've covered your sisters, but there were a lot of kids who went through here over the years. I'm sure they'd like to pay their respects."

Her face relaxed a fraction. "That would be amazing. I'm sure we'll have a houseful after the funeral, but I need a chance to gird my loins for the influx. Mom kept a list. I'll get it for you."

As she disappeared upstairs, he wandered into the living room. Little had changed over the years. The big, cushy sofas had rotated a time or two. And there'd been at least three rugs that he could remember. But photos of Joan and her charges were scattered everywhere. Xander eased along the wall, scanning faces. A lot of them he knew. A lot of them, he didn't.

A shot at the end caught his attention. The girl's face was turned away from the camera, looking out over the misty mountains. She was on the cusp of womanhood, her long, tanned legs crossed on the swing that still hung from the porch outside, a book forgotten in her lap. Her golden hair was caught in a loose tail at her nape. Xander's fingers itched with the memory of the silky strands flowing through his fingers. She'd been sixteen, gorgeous, and the center of his world. The sight of her still gave him a punch in the gut.

"Here it is."

At the sound of Pru's voice, Xander turned away from Kennedy's picture. *Over and done.*

He strode over and took the pages she'd printed. "I'll take care of it," he promised.

"Thank you, Xander. This means a lot."

"Anytime." With one last, affectionate tug on her hair, he stepped outside, away from memories and the looming specter of what might have been.

∿

GET your copy of *When You Got A Good Thing* today!

OTHER BOOKS BY KAIT NOLAN

A complete and up-to-date list of all my books can be found at https://kaitnolan.com.

- *Stirred Up by a SEAL* (Jonah and Rachel)
- *Hung Up on the Hacker* (Cash and Hadley)
- *Caught Up with the Captain* (Grey and Rebecca)

RESCUE MY HEART SERIES
SMALL TOWN MILITARY ROMANCE

- *Baby It's Cold Outside* (Ivy and Harrison)
- *What I Like About You* (Laurel and Sebastian)
- *Bad Case of Loving You* (Paisley and Ty prequel)
- *Made For Loving You* (Paisley and Ty)

THE MISFIT INN SERIES
SMALL TOWN FAMILY ROMANCE

- *When You Got A Good Thing* (Kennedy and Xander)
- *Til There Was You* (Misty and Denver)
- *Those Sweet Words* (Pru and Flynn)
- *Stay A Little Longer* (Athena and Logan)
- *Bring It On Home* (Maggie and Porter)

MEN OF THE MISFIT INN
SMALL TOWN SOUTHERN ROMANCE

- *Let It Be Me* (Emerson and Caleb)
- *Our Kind of Love* (Abbey and Kyle)
- *Don't You Wanna Stay* (Deanna and Wyatt)
- *Until We Meet Again* (Samantha and Griffin prequel)
- *Come A Little Closer* (Samantha and Griffin)
- *Just Wanted You To Know* (Livia and Declan): April 14

WISHFUL ROMANCE SERIES
SMALL TOWN SOUTHERN ROMANCE

- *Once Upon A Coffee* (Avery and Dillon)
- *To Get Me To You* (Cam and Norah)
- *Know Me Well* (Liam and Riley)
- *Be Careful, It's My Heart* (Brody and Tyler)
- *Just For This Moment* (Myles and Piper)
- *Wish I Might* (Reed and Cecily)
- *Turn My World Around* (Tucker and Corinne)
- *Dance Me A Dream* (Jace and Tara)
- *See You Again* (Trey and Sandy)
- *The Christmas Fountain* (Chad and Mary Alice)
- *You Were Meant For Me* (Mitch and Tess)
- *A Lot Like Christmas* (Ryan and Hannah)
- *Dancing Away With My Heart* (Zach and Lexi)

WISHING FOR A HERO SERIES (A WISHFUL SPINOFF SERIES)
SMALL TOWN ROMANTIC SUSPENSE

- *Make You Feel My Love* (Judd and Autumn)
- *Watch Over Me* (Nash and Rowan)
- *Can't Take My Eyes Off You* (Ethan and Miranda)
- *Burn For You* (Sean and Delaney)

MEET CUTE ROMANCE
SMALL TOWN SHORT ROMANCE

- *Once Upon A Snow Day*
- *Once Upon A New Year's Eve*
- *Once Upon An Heirloom*
- *Once Upon A Coffee*
- *Once Upon A Campfire*
- *Once Upon A Rescue*

SUMMER CAMP
CONTEMPORARY ROMANCE

- *Once Upon A Campfire*
- *Second Chance Summer*

ABOUT KAIT

Kait is a Mississippi native, who often swears like a sailor, calls everyone sugar, honey, or darlin', and can wield a bless your heart like a saber or a Snuggie, depending on requirements.

You can find more information on this *USA Today* best selling and RITA ® Award-winning author and her books on her website http://kaitnolan.com. While you're there, sign up for her newsletter so you don't miss out on news about new releases!